DUSTY ROAD HOME

DUSTY ROAD HOME

ISABELLA

SAPPHIRE BOOKS

SALINAS, CALIFORNIA

Dedication

The the love of my life!

Chapter One

Mel hung her head out the window and let the sun beat down on her. She wanted to enjoy what was left of the autumn warmth. She'd spent so much time in the sun lately that her freckles were poppin' like it was the middle of summer, but it was okay. She didn't need to worry about her appearance anymore. Max laid his head on her leg and sprawled out on the bench seat of the truck. He'd adjusted well to the country life, too well in fact. He found joy chasing chickens, and if she didn't know better, he was a cow wrangler in a former life.

She took a deep breath. The smell of cut hay filled the air just as a bug splattered on her face.

"Jesus Christ," she said, twisting the rearview mirror toward her so she could wipe the guts off her cheek. "Fucking bugs."

Whop, whop, whop.

Pfff.

Mel closed her eyes and sighed. Why did God have to take a beautiful day and turn it to crap? She looked around her as she heard the distinct sound of a flat tire. She tried to see which side of the truck the sound was coming from. Looking back through the window, sure enough, she'd lost a tire. Pulling off the road, she slid off the seat, her cowboy boots kicking up dust as she slammed the truck door.

"Stay, Max," she said, pointing to the seat. She

wasn't in the mood to chase him in the event he saw a prairie dog. She wasn't sure, but she could almost swear he tossed her a smile as he laid his head out the open window.

Mel kicked the flat tire. "God dammit. Couldn't you just give me twenty more miles till I got into town?"

Slipping under the truck, she dropped the spare and jack onto the dirt so she could change the threadbare tire.

The sound of a car passing by made Mel twist under the truck and watch as the driver slammed on the brakes and came back in reverse. They got little traffic this far out, so another car on the road made her pay attention.

"Hey. Can you help a girl out?"

Mel looked sideways from under the truck, spotting a set of feet in sandals standing next to her jeans and boots. The word *contrast* popped into her mind. No one dressed like that out here, so she had to be a lost tourist looking for the ever-elusive ball of twine, trucks punched into the scorched desert, or some other tourist trap. She definitely wasn't one of those tree-huggers Mel had seen often in town, their backpacks covered in state park patches, water bottles hanging down and bumping off slender, short-clad thighs. Oh, how easily her mind wandered to those girls who wore short-shorts and hiking boots.

"Sure, what can I do ya?" she said, scooting out from under the pickup. She slipped her cowboy hat on and pushed it low, just above her sunglasses. Mel couldn't help but give the woman a once-over. Tan, fit, and feminine was her type—if she even had a type anymore. Women should come with warning stickers like "drama queen" or "shit show."

She kept her back to the woman and dusted herself off.

"Christ." Looking at the spare tire, it wasn't any better than the one she was taking off. Getting new tires had slipped her mind when the water heater blew. The coming winter wasn't the time of year you wanted to be without a water heater. Then again, when one lived so far out in the sticks and UPS and mail service refused to deliver heavy items, transportation was a smidge more important. Hell, if she needed to, she could've dipped water from the trough for a sponge bath.

"Well, sir, I'm looking for …thirteen Old Wire Road."

Double shit.

"Huh." Mel rolled the tire to the side of the truck and leaned it against the body. Slipping the lug wrench on the nut, she cranked down on it, barely budging the damn thing.

"Do you know where it is or not?"

Mel gave a sideways glance toward the Mercedes she drove up in. Black, a 200 Sport Coupe. The big brass Coach emblem between the toes of her sandals and flowing Vera Wang sundress all spelled money to Mel. They screamed, "Look at me." It was hard to not notice the way the sundress danced around her body. *Damn, she's soft on the eyes.*

"I do, but you won't find anyone out there."

"How do you know?" She peeked between the sunglasses and floppy brim of her sun hat.

"They left for town. Probably won't be back for hours, if they didn't go out of town, that is."

"Shit."

"You probably should have called before making the trek out so far."

"Funny guy. I would call, but her number isn't listed. I'm on a deadline. Christ." The woman slapped down her flowing dress that was threatening to blow up around her waist. Mel was rooting for the wind. At least then the flat tire would be offset by something entertaining.

"Huh." Mel finished, pulling the lug nuts and dropping them into the hubcap with a clank. Jerking up and down on the jack, she lifted the old truck to one side and spun the tire, making sure it was clear of the ground.

"Jesus Christ, why does this always happen to me? Another fucking goose chase looking for Melanie Crenshaw. Why do I always get the reclusive, unstable assholes?"

Mel bent her head down lower, tempted to spout off, but she just kept working on changing the spare. So, the woman was on a mission. Too bad; she wouldn't mind engaging the woman further, but her then secret would be revealed, and Mel wasn't in the mood to explain why she'd left the big city and come home for some peace.

"Do you know Melanie Crenshaw?"

"Heard of her, but I don't...nope."

"Hmm. Of course you don't. I'm out here in the boonies and no one knows anyone. I wouldn't be surprised if I started hearing banjo music any minute."

Mel frowned at the comment. She didn't consider her hometown to be a parody of a movie. They might not be as enlightened as the liberal big city, but they weren't hicks either. Jesus, why did people stereotype small towns? "We all pretty much keep to ourselves out here, ma'am."

"Of course you do." The woman stepped back as Mel hoisted the busted tire and threw it in the bed. As Mel slapped at her pants, the woman stepped back farther, clearly worried her off-yellow spring dress would be a dirt magnet.

"Well, if you hear of Melanie Crenshaw or know someone who might know her, can you call me? I would really appreciate it." She handed Mel her business card.

Mel fanned the card between her fingers. "She owe you money or something?"

"No." Pilar was too focused on her phone as she answered. "I just wanted to chat with her. Do you get phone service out here? I can't seem to get a signal." Pilar lifted her phone and turned in a small circle.

"Well, if you get closer to town, you'll get a signal. It's kinda spotty out here."

"Of course it is. Damn." Pilar gave her a quick once-over and then looked at her phone again, dismissing Mel's very presence.

Mel examined the card closer. A dirty thumbprint was planted next to the name: Pilar Stein. Mel studied the woman again. The name rang a bell, but Mel couldn't put her finger on why. Well, that was a dichotomy. She didn't exactly look like a Pilar, but then she didn't look like a Stein either.

"If you see her, can you pass on my business card and let her know I'll be in town for a few days?"

"Sure."

"Great, thanks." Pilar strolled back to her car, cursing under her breath. "Cute dog, by the way."

Mel didn't respond to the comment. Instead, she was mesmerized by the sundress floating around the woman as she flounced off. The last view was the way the dress hugged her ass as she walked away.

"Too bad," she muttered as she slipped off her work gloves and slapped them against her thigh. Covering her eyes, she checked the location of the sun. It was still high, and she had a good few hours more of daylight. Enough to get to town and back with another load of lumber, feed, and a new water heater. "Well, I hope you find what you're looking for, ma'am," Mel said to the receding taillights. Panic and anxiety raced through her She didn't like being the center of attention, and a reporter snooping around town could be dangerous for her and her family.

Mel pulled her hat off her head and ran her fingers through her newly shorn tresses, suddenly thankful for the new look and weight loss. She wouldn't recommend the breakup diet, but if it was just weight that she had to worry about, Mel would take it. It was clear that the woman had mistaken her for a man.

Tucking the business card into her jeans, she slid into the driver's seat, kicked the column shift down, and tried not to peel out. The more distance she put between her and the stranger, the better she'd feel. Besides, her stomach was growling and one of George's burgers sounded great right about now. Looking in her rearview mirror, she tried to watch the Mercedes barrel down the road before it was completely out of sight. She suspected she hadn't seen the last of the woman in the yellow spring dress with the sun-drenched skin.

Max leaned against the passenger door and poked his head out of the window. The wind ruffled his mouth open as he tried to bite at the current. He was the best company she could hope for, and she couldn't imagine life without him.

Mel suspected what the hound wanted was a lunge around the county. She wasn't in the right frame of mind to talk about the reasons she'd run from the city to the country, so she was glad Max couldn't talk. No, Mel didn't need reminding, as she thought about it every damn day. It haunted her dreams. Every free moment it crowded out other thoughts, torturing her on an endless loop of that week. Crushing longing was a constant companion everywhere she went, so no, she didn't want to talk to Pilar Stein about anything. The woman's card didn't say "reporter" or sport a publication logo, but Mel had heard the way she'd said "deadline" and knew that she was on some sort of journalistic beat. Mel had always been extremely guarded about her private life, granting interviews only when her literary agent insisted it was necessary to promote her latest book. But she drew the line when it came to talking about her personal life, and that wasn't about to change anytime soon. Unfortunately, despite leaving the city to escape the prying eyes of cell phone cameras and gossip chasers, she wasn't in full control of what people might say about her. While the relationship—and breakup— with Jill Steele had all been on the down low, that didn't mean that people who knew would keep her secret. Especially Jill's husband, who had made it his mission to confront her.

He'd found her at the quiet, tucked-away coffee shop that served as her second office and self-imposed time-out place where there was always a discarded daily paper for distraction. The only other person who knew about the place was her assistant. So how did he accidentally show up?

Her head buried in her computer, she hadn't noticed the man standing in front of her, his arms crossed and his face a study in poorly controlled anger management.

Without looking up, she said, "Can I help you?"

He didn't say a word. Instead, he dropped an envelope on her laptop and waited.

Mel picked it up; its heft was deceiving. Several pictures slid out from the cramped space they'd been shoved into. She didn't need to take them all out if these were any indication of what was left inside.

"How much do you want?" It was always about money. This wasn't her first blackmail scheme, and she was sure if she continued to be out in the public eye, there would be more. It was one of the reasons she'd tried to keep her relationship with Jill such a secret.

"I don't want your fucking money. I want my wife back."

Shit. Shit. Shit.

"I have no idea what you're talking about." Mel resisted the urge to look at the man. Luckily the coffee shop was almost empty, somewhere between the morning grind and the liquid lunch crowd. It was her favorite time of day.

"Please leave." Mel ordered.

"I'm not going anywhere. You and me are gonna have a talk and get this shit settled."

A shower of photos cascaded across her computer and the table, some landing on the floor.

"Does this ring a bell?" The man shoved a particularly explicit photo under her nose. "Look at it."

Mel glanced up at the man, his face enraged, the blood vessels in his neck and face bulging. "If you don't leave, I'll be forced to call the police, Mister..."

"You know who the fuck I am, bitch." He picked up a handful of photos and threw, many hitting Mel in the face. "Don't come around my wife again, or you'll be sorry. She's mine and always will be," he said, leaning down and menacingly whispering in Mel's ear.

What was it about men who viewed all the women in their lives like possessions? She'd had enough of the entitled prick. "You should probably talk to Jill and find out why she would leave such a fine specimen of toxic masculinity. Then again, I think you could probably answer that question for her, couldn't you?"

Mel stood, and just as she did, he grabbed her by the neck, practically lifting her off her feet. She clawed at the fingers cutting off her life, but he only tightened. Without thinking, she jerked her knee forward and hit him square in the balls. His grip lessened a fraction when she raked his face with her fingernails. The barista came around the corner and laced his beefy arm around his neck and took him to the ground. Wrapping his legs around the idiot's midsection, he held him until the man passed out.

"Nice work," Mel said as the kid rolled the man off him.

"Thanks. I'm hoping for a tryout with the MMA and...well, you never know when those skills will come in handy."

"No kidding," Mel said, rubbing her throat.

"Are you okay? I called the cops."

"Yeah, he didn't like my last book, so he wanted a refund."

Mel tried to laugh, but her throat hurt. She took a sip of her coffee and swallowed hard past the pain.

She gathered up all the photos and tucked them back into the envelope, which she put in her pocket.

"Aw, the police are here." The bright flashing lights filled the room. "I'll bring you another coffee. I'm sure they'll want to talk to both of us," the kid said, stating the obvious.

After Mel gave her statement, she'd pulled out her phone to call Jill. She'd glossed over the attempted strangling but firmly suggested they take a break for a while, at least until things cooled down and she could put some distance between Jill and her husband. Clearly, Jill disagreed, protesting vehemently. It wasn't a request, at least not for Mel. She knew they were finished at that point, and while she loved Jill, being involved with someone who had a toxic ex was drama she didn't need in her life at the moment. It had taken weeks for Mel to come to terms with the decision she'd made about Jill; damn, the sex had been good. If only Jill had taken a graceful exit. The flowers, the cards, a plane ticket to Rome…all ways Jill thought she'd try to win Mel over. She'd even stopped by the coffeehouse to catch Mel when she, too, discovered her sanctuary, but after the incident with Jill's husband, Mel hired a protection detail for a couple of weeks. They had kept Jill at bay and then immediately recommended a change to her routine, which meant, unfortunately, that the coffee shop was out as a second office and she'd have to read her newspaper elsewhere.

Suddenly, the name hit her. Pilar Stein was a Pulitzer-winning reporter.

Max leaned against Mel and rested his head on her thigh. "So, what is a reporter of her stature doing searching me out? Huh, Max?" She stroked his head as he looked up at her.

Now she wasn't so sure she'd put her past behind her.

Max jumped up and licked her face and leaned against her "Huh?" she said again, running her hand down his fur and gently slapping his hind quarter. "Sometimes the shit you bury in your past doesn't stay buried. It's not like those bones you take to the backyard, buddy. Yes, she's attractive, but she's trouble, Max. Trust me, she's up to no good."

She'd run to the solace of her hometown, trading the big city for the gentle rolling hills of her childhood. The laid-back country life had always called to her, and when her mother was alive it was where she came when she needed someone to talk to, so it always held a special place in her heart. While others felt like they could never go home, for her home was and would also be here. God, how she wished she could pick up the phone and talk to her mom just one more time. She fought back the urge to cry for what she'd lost when her mother died. Then something hit her: maybe she was here for a different reason.

"Shit."

She thought about giving her dad a call and a heads-up, then quickly dismissed the idea.

"I don't owe him shit," she said, burying her head against Max's. "Let him deal with the nosy reporter on his own."

It was just a hunch, but her suspicions weren't usually wrong.

"Let's go get a burger and think about this, buddy." She cranked on the wheel and guided the old pickup back onto the road to town. She needed to think about this new development. Somehow she knew that the reporter was out for a big story and her life was just about to get interesting.

※ ※ ※ ※

An hour later, George's had proven to be a bust. His usual cook was replaced with some kid who didn't seem to know how a burger should be cooked. The almost fresh onions were soft and buttery, and the bun had scorch marks on it that would make her dad proud, but the patty...well his lack of years showed in the near raw meat staring back at her. She gave the inedible burger to Max instead.

"The burnt parts are good for your teeth," her dad had said when she complained about the constantly charred offerings he laid on her plate as a kid. While some fathers had a knack for grilling, hers...well, he just couldn't get it down, even when she'd remodeled his whole backyard with a grilling island his buddies drooled over.

Her new water tank rattled between the stacks of lumber, chicken feed, and a bale of hay.

"It better not bust," she said, looking over at Max, ruffling the fur on his head. All she wanted was a hot shower, sleep, and some quiet time, but that would have to wait until after she sorted out the tire situation. At least she knew Mike would put her first in line at the garage—one of the perks of small-town living. She didn't regret tossing away all the big city offered—the vestiges of the corner coffee shops, fancy restaurants, bumper-to-bumper traffic, all replaced for the simple life. She knew she would have traded it all in eventually, but the potential of a nasty scandal and bad breakup just made it happen sooner than expected. Now, she worried her past was revisiting her with the arrival of the woman in the Mercedes.

Chapter Two

Well, he was no help." Pilar stared in her rearview mirror as the truck pulled farther away. She pulled off the road and looked at the map laid out on the seat. She twisted this way and that. How could she have found herself so hopelessly lost? "Cute dog, though."

She picked up the folder she'd created on Melanie Crenshaw.

"I have a fucking Pulitzer. What the hell am I doing in the middle of nowhere trying to track down someone who ditched life for the snail's pace of this cow town?"

She picked up the few photos she'd been able to find of the woman. Attractive, yet something in her eyes were haunting Pilar. The photos were years old, and the most recent one was a publicity shot for one of her earlier novels. They were all she could find on short notice. The woman avoided the press like bats avoid the sun. She thumbed through the press clippings, all without a current photo, the bulk of the articles about her books being optioned for a series of movies. It was the best her editor could do as she tossed the job on Pilar's desk. The gossip around her sudden departure from her home in the city had been interesting and challenging enough for Magdalena to toss it Pilar's way. Maybe it was her tenacity that convinced her? Then again, maybe it was Pilar's constant hounding that had finally broken down her editor's resolve. Magdalena had expressed her doubts about Pilar's ability to deliver on this story, and now Pilar was regretting being so pushy.

Rumors—whispers, really—of lesbianism, plagiarism, and every other ism out there swirled around the author. None of it came from credible sources, so until she had proof she would just have to try to find it for herself. Besides, what was the big deal if the woman was gay? Hadn't the world moved past the issue? Obviously not, if Melanie Crenshaw had taken to hiding in her hometown. Or could it be that her family had drawn her back?

Pilar picked up the photo of Lauden Crenshaw, another author who suddenly fell off the face of the earth about a decade back and just happened to be the father of one Melanie Crenshaw. A skyrocketing career that came to a screeching halt. Maybe it was a familial thing. Success wasn't for everyone, and some lost their way when the limelight and money started rolling in. Lauden had a fatherly look to him and yet he was as elusive as his daughter. Her phone calls to him had gone unanswered, not surprisingly. His fellow authors though didn't have the same problem talking about Lauden. A mix of jealousy and resentment were evident with everyone she'd talked to about the man. And they said journalism could be a vicious career choice.

Pilar shook her head in frustration. She should be covering the latest Washington scandal. With a new crop of politicians taking office, there was no shortage of intriguing stories to pick from. The Pulitzer should have opened a bunch of doors for her—and it had. But the lasting trauma from the very story that had garnered the top accolade just wouldn't let her go. She'd tried talk therapy, support groups, even hypnosis, but no remedy for the next two years had freed her of her overwhelming PTSD and anxiety. And fear was the number one enemy of any investigative reporter worth their salt.

Pilar finally hit on something that worked—a therapist she liked and self-defense training workouts several times a week. Bolstered by a new sense of strength and self-confidence, she'd been picking up the pieces, taking every minor freelance piece that came her way just to keep her head in the game. Certainly, with enough puff pieces under her belt, she'd make herself ready for a real story. Someday.

The *Literary Times* was one step closer to the hard-hitting investigative stories she'd churned out in the runup to the Pulitzer. It wasn't the *New York Times*—yet—but it was what she could handle at the moment and had way more legitimacy than a tabloid or online "entertainment news" outlet. Besides, Magdalena, the editor that shepherded the Pulitzer-winning article, had moved over to the *Literary Times* and had done Pilar a favor by putting her on stories at all. So, she'd pay her dues tracking down a reclusive woman who definitely didn't want to be found, and use her charm to tease out exclusive information for the in-depth profile her editor wanted. If she could just catch a break…the town was too small for nobody to know nothing about nothing. She was confident that her reporter's nose could sniff out the answer eventually. There was too much riding on this story for her, and she would be damned if Melanie Crenshaw would evade her.

Pilar looked at Melanie's press photos again. She

was definitely attractive and had that kind of guess-my-orientation look about her. The eyes, though, they…well, they seemed so…what was the word she was looking for?

Sad.

The polar opposite of the photo of her father. His beaming, cat-who-ate-the-canary smile gave him a sort of arrogant air. He was definitely someone who seemed to enjoy the spotlight if his press photo was any indication of the type of man he was. So why did Melanie Crenshaw seem so lost? Yep, two total opposites, yet from the same tree. The more she wondered the more she wanted to get to the bottom of why Melanie had gone off the social and media grid, so to speak.

"Back to town, I guess." Tossing the folder on the seat, she tried to refold the useless paper guide she'd picked up at the gas station when she realized she had no cell service and the GPS app stopped working. She tossed the redneck origami in the seat behind her. Tapping her phone again, she strained to look at her destination on the map app, but it was useless. It was as if all the roads ended somewhere, just not the road she was looking for.

"Of course, GPS isn't working out here in hell's playground." She shaded her eyes and looked around the vast expanse of wide-open spaces. The only living things were the black specks that moved every once in a while and dotted the gently rolling hills studded with trees. She'd figured out they were cows—at least she thought they were cows. She'd passed a large, foul-smelling farm getting off the highway. The beasts were packed in pens and the odor almost made her vomit. Seeing a group of men herding the bovines, she couldn't believe that people lived and worked around that smell twenty-four hours a day, every day.

❧ ❧ ❧ ❧

Pilar circled back into the driveway of the burger joint. God, all she wanted was a diet soda and air conditioning.

George's Drive-In was plastered across a sign that had probably seen its heyday in the fifties.

Walking inside, Pilar felt like she'd stepped back a few decades and into a world that looked more like a car-hop movie set in the 1950s. She stepped around the hanging fly strip, coated in flies. The smell of bacon lingered in the air, making her hungry. A burger would be nice right about now. A protein bar was breakfast, and it hadn't lasted long this morning.

Squinting at the menu, she could make out a loaded burger and fries. "Four fifty," she muttered.

"Yep, soda's extra. No refills, but iced tea is all you can drink," a rotund man shouted from behind the opening to the kitchen. "Margie, get your ass out here. You gotta customer."

Silence.

"Must be on a smoke break." He walked around from the kitchen, wiping his hands on his stained apron. "What can I get ya?'

"Are you George?"

"I am." George rubbed the scruff on his chin with the handle of the spatula.

"Hey, you wouldn't happen to know Melanie Crenshaw, would you?"

"Ol' Mel? Sure, you just missed her."

"Are you kidding?" Pilar looked out into the

parking lot. "Christ, just my luck. What kinda car is she driving?" Maybe Pilar passed her leaving.

"No car. Pickup. Old Ford. Said something about needing to get tires on it. Got a flat today."

"No shit?" She couldn't believe she'd just been talking to the one person who could've led her to Mel Crenshaw: Mel Crenshaw herself.

"Yep, you a friend of Mel's?"

"Sorta."

"Do you want to order?"

Pilar looked at the menu. She knew she shouldn't, but what the hell. She'd do extra Zumba next week.

Chapter Three

The auto shop was a small but busy place.. Cars might have been its meat and potatoes, but that didn't stop people from bringing in their mowers, tractors, weed whackers, and leaf blowers. If it had an engine in it, it came to Mike's. In a small town, if your engine started to go there weren't many places to turn to, especially when mechanics were in short supply, opting for better paying jobs in the city.

So, Mike made sure to get his hands in a bit of everything.

Right now, his hands were occupied with a thin paper cup filled with steaming, dark roast coffee. It smelled rank and bitter, too strong for Mel's tastes, but she took one when he offered it up to her all the same. It never paid to be rude to the person who was fixing your car.

Mike said, "Been a while since you've been in here."

"I know. Been a while since I needed something fixed." Mel patted Max's head as he leaned against her leg.

"Can't stop by to chat anymore?" Mike knelt down and ruffled Max's fur. "You need to bring Mommy to the shop more often, Max."

Max leaned into the rough petting, his tongue hanging out at all the attention.

Traitor. Mel thought, watching her dog bond

with Mike.

"You know it's not like that, Mike."

"Sure, sure, it's never like that. Always got a ton of good reasons why you don't want to see me." His off-center grin was kind and sincere. He was quite a few years older than Mel, with a crooked nose that had been broken a few times too many. "You ever think that maybe it would get you a discount if you brought me coffee once in a while?"

Mel held up her paper cup. "Is that you admitting that this is bad?"

"No." Mike snorted. "That there is the best damn coffee in the county. It can't be beat by no other brew. I was just using it as an example. Stopping by for more than tires occasionally might be nice." She'd known Mike had a crush on her for a while. He'd made a trip out to the farm, on the guise of lending a hand, when he found out her tractor had blown a tire.

"I know, I know," relented Mel. She really hadn't been a good friend or neighbor lately. She ran a hand through her hair, pushing it back out of her face. "I've just been busy. It's no excuse, but with that winter storm about to come in..."

Mike gave a low whistle through his teeth. "All right, I'll let you off the hook with that one. It is looking to be a bit of a doozy. Your first winter back in town, and you're about to get snowed in good. That's got to be something."

"It's a little nerve-racking," admitted Mel. "I'm still trying to get used to being back here, you know? And the farm...it's got a lot of work to be done on it still. The winter's going to be a beast to get through."

"But you'll be here for the holidays. That's something."

"It sure is." Mel wasn't sure if it was a good something yet or a bad something, but she could agree that it was something. She asked, "Got any plans for the holiday, Mike?"

Mike gave her a long, amiable smile. He stepped around the side of the counter and over an empty gasoline tin that had been knocked onto its side. The shop itself was small, the main entrance connecting the office to the shop portion. There was a single door leading into the checkout bay, and a rolling tin door that led into the garage. Another door connected the two.

Mike led her over to one of the pictures hanging on the garage wall. He tapped it with his finger. "I'm taking the boys out to the cabin."

"The boys" were Mike's best friends, Theo and George. They had all been held back the same year in high school and bonded over a hatred for sitting still in class and a love of hunting. Last Mel heard, Theo was actually out of town at the moment, chasing after some sweetheart of his.

Surprised, she asked, "Theo's coming back?"

"Comes back every winter," Mike said. "Wouldn't miss being home for the holidays." He caught himself, adding on, "Just the way he is. Likes me taking him to the cabin too much for that."

It only stung a bit. People tried not to give Mel too much flack for having been gone so long. She came back when it was important, even if it was a little too late. "I think that sounds like fun. What's the backup plan?"

"Backup plan?"

"You know. In case the weather gets too bad."

Mike laughed. "We're counting on the weather

being bad. The goal is to get ourselves snowed into that cabin, so we've got an excuse to stay longer for the weekend. It's going to be the three of us, a deck of cards, and—"

"All the beer you can drink?"

"All the beer we can drink. Well, maybe not. Depends. Theo's on-again, off-again sober. If he's not drinking right now, we won't bring it along." Mike downed half his coffee and then made a face. "But it'll be good either way. It's less about getting shit-faced and more about getting to catch up, you know?"

"Yeah, I've sure enjoyed that about being home. I'll say that much. I wanted to swing by Jenna's place before winter hit, but—"

"You can always join us out at the cabin if you want. It'll be fun. Just like old times." Mike offered her a wide grin. Yep, he was sweet on her, and it was making her uncomfortable. It hadn't been a secret that she was gay, but it wasn't front page news, at least not here.

"Thanks, Mike. I promised my dad that I'd go out and see him and spend the holidays with him." It wasn't strictly true, but she had every intention to call her father at some point. "Ever since my mom…well, I just figured it might be nice if I showed up for once."

He bumped her shoulder against his and nodded. "I get it. No worries, maybe next time."

She felt like she'd dodged a bullet, for now. "Next time, for sure." It wasn't a promise she'd keep, and she hoped by then he'd get the hint.

"Jenna will probably have already left by now, I reckon. I don't get that having split houses thing."

"I guess when you can afford it, you use it," Mel said with a shrug. She didn't want to acknowledge she was in the same boat, but she could understand Jenna wanting to get away from the gossip incubator that sometimes felt like a prison more than a refuge. Jenna was an old friend, but not the best. She had made it big about ten years back when stock trading changed and everyone with a computer could be a day trader, and she'd been acting like she owned the Ritz ever since.

Her farm was the one farthest at the edge of town, a good drive no matter what, with about seven hundred acres. Inherited—like a lot of the places in the area—it had been in Jenna's family for almost five generations now.

Mike asked, "Speaking of houses, how's yours coming along?"

"Oh, you know," Mel said noncommittally.

Mike snorted. "That don't tell me nothing. And I'm not looking for Miss Perfection here either. I know you've got high standards. I'm talking about practical."

"I still don't have the hot water heater fixed."

"But those fuses?"

"I got them all switched out and replaced the box. Got the outlet fixed too."

"That's good," Mike said. "It's a good start. You can't move into a place like that and expect it to be ready and raring to go in a few months' time. It's not bad. I've driven by it a few times. Not recently, mind you, but back while it was sitting empty. Seems like the foundation is still good on it, and the porch ain't rotted through."

Mel had made her fair share of trips back home for months looking for the perfect ranch to buy. When the O'Donnell ranch came up for sale, she'd driven back four separate times to check things out. If she were honest with herself, the prospect of moving back home was like snuggling down in that warm comfy bed after a long day at work, curling up under the family quilt and burying your head underneath to avoid the mythical monster that lived under the bed. She chuckled at the simile. Was her dad the beast and she had to face him, or was she romanticizing her childhood town? It didn't matter, she missed the small-town feel, the opportunity to reconnect with friends she'd left behind, and the opportunity to put down roots someplace that held memories of her mother. God how she missed her mom, and she hoped moving back would give her a bit of peace mentally and spiritually. She'd run away as soon as her mom died and hadn't looked back, but now she felt an urgency to settle things with her family. She wasn't holding her breath that her father would be open to that, the selfish prick. Still, he was family, and she would do her part even if he wouldn't.

"Yeah, well, I've only really been back for a month, but I'm sure I can get it in shape before winter sets in. I've missed this place, and I'm glad to be home." Mel leaned against her truck. "Front porch isn't bad, but there's rot on the back porch. So, I've got a call in to Andy to help me around the place, so things should move quicker with help. Lumber in the back of the truck is for the back stairs."

"Back porch doesn't matter half as much though, does it? No one's going to be standing around on the back porch. The front is the heart of the house."

"I thought those were the windows?"

Mike guffawed and slapped at his thigh like it was the funniest thing he'd ever heard. He shook his head, taking a moment to get the breath back in himself before saying, "Nah. The windows are the eyes. The front porch is the heart. First thing anyone sees when they go by, and the spot that welcomes you in at the end of the day."

"When did you get so poetic?"

Mike shrugged. "I've been trying a few new things."

"What, really?"

"My hands are getting bad on me. I won't be able to do this job forever. Besides, I think it's time to work smarter, not harder. I ain't ready for retirement, but if you can't hold a wrench and crank down on an engine…well, I don't want that on my conscience. Besides, I know the missus is ready to have me underfoot every day." Mike flexed his hands, the gnarled fingers not straightening. A shop accident in high school had almost crushed his hands completely. That was the end of the mechanics program and the start of the long, drawn-out lawsuit his parents had filed against the school district. "Besides, Leo's thinking about moving outta town once he's done with high school."

Leo was one of the local kids. He was a good guy, and he'd been working around the shop since he was twelve. Sweeping and cleanup work to begin with, but he'd been learning a thing or two about the mechanical end of things lately. It was always sad to see when someone was moving on. Mel wondered sometimes if that's how people felt when she moved away.

It was something of a betrayal to everyone here, and if she dwelled too much, it left a nasty taste in her mouth. She quickly asked, "What's he moving on for?"

"Trucker work, or maybe join the Army. He wants to drive. Getting ready to apply for the right license and all. Won't be able to get his own rig right away, but he knows someone that's looking for a riding partner. Thinks it will help put more food on the table than the work he does here. Don't blame him, mind you. We don't get the same sort of work around here that we used to. Just seems like I'll need to find someone else to take over or maybe I'll just sell the shop. He tells me the Army offers him some of the same opportunities, a steady paycheck, with benefits. I'm trying to talk him into staying, but he's gonna be a man pretty soon, so he'll do his own thing. If he leaves, I won't have no one to help with the heavy lifting, so…"

Clearly, he was either going to have to find another young kid looking for a skill, or shut down the shop. People talked about houses and humans passing away in old towns, but it was businesses that died the most. Their owners got old and ended up with no kids who wanted to take on the business afterward. The main street in town was practically a graveyard at this point.

Mel was pretty sure that the only two places in town that could never go out would be the grocers and the feed store. Business never faltered at those places, even in the hard times, like in the dead of a winter. People and animals alike always needed to eat.

"I bet you'll find someone else," Mel said. "Kids around here are always looking for work."

"Sure, but I need someone with a good head on their shoulders. I can't have any meathead thinking they can come in here, throw around a few tools, and walk away on top. It's rough trade work." That's how most country folk viewed things like mechanics and electric work. You had to apprentice under someone first, or there was no point wasting the money to hire you.

Mel asked, "Didn't Dodie have a kid that was interested in cars?"

"Who, Shelby?" Mike hummed. "I haven't spoken to Dodie in ages. I don't know if her girl is still looking for something."

"Might be worth a try." Mel had long suspected the girl might be family, but you didn't out someone unless they came to you and told you themselves. People were really cautious about those kinds of assumptions, except for the hen parties where gossip and innuendo passed for entertainment, a currency almost better than money in a remote town.

"Might be," Mike replied. "And you changed the subject. We aren't talking about the garage. We're talking about the house. Got the fuses taken care of. Got plans for the socket. What are you going to do about that water tank, Mel? You can't leave it sitting around broke all winter. We'll end up pulling you frozen from the house come the end of the storm season."

"I'm working on it. I got a new one in the back of the truck right now, see? So, don't worry, it's all good."

"Seems more like you're putting off working on it, if you ask me. Should've been the first thing that you tore apart," Mike said. "Everything comes after the hot water and heat, you should know that. Especially with this storm getting ready to come in. You don't want to end up stuck cold all winter."

Mel nodded. She was about to respond when

she heard the sound of tires on the loose gravel outside. She looked out through the garage door, and her heart skipped a beat when she saw the reporter's car. Without thinking about how it would look, she charged forward, grabbing onto the rolling metal door and slamming it down.

"What the hell are you doing?"

"Heading out," Mel said. "If someone comes in here asking for me, tell them I've hitched a ride back to the farm."

Baffled, Mike asked, "What are you going on about?"

"Just do it, Mike, please?" She gave him a wide-eyed stare.

"All right, all right, but you're going to explain this later."

Mel threw her arms around him in a hug. "You're the best."

She ducked into the office just as someone knocked on the rolling door. Mel closed her eyes, waiting until she heard the metal door rattle up.

This was the perfect time for Mel to make her escape and dodge Pilar Stein, quietly exiting out the back. Mel thought about walking back to the ranch but decided that the best change of plans would be to go hide out at the diner for a while and come back to the garage later to pick up her truck. It wouldn't take Mike more than an hour to get the tires all changed out. The trick would be biding enough time until Pilar had left.

Mel started the walk back into town.

"Come on, Max. Let's go get an edible burger this time. What do you say, buddy? Hmm?"

She didn't want to go home. She didn't want

to deal with whatever mess Pilar Stein was trying to bring into her life. The thing was, Mel had enough on her plate. Life had gotten wild on her, and it had gotten wild on her fast. She didn't want to spend her days playing hide-and-seek with some reporter that was shoving her nose where it didn't belong.

At the beginning of her career, her agent had given Mel "the talk" the minute the woman found out Mel was a lesbian. She explained that Mel being out would dilute her success and take the focus off her writing.

Dilute?

What was that?

According to her agent, she needed to keep her personal life just that: personal. The mystery genre was a male-dominated category, and women had a hard enough time breaking through the paper ceiling. Add homophobia to that and Mel could practically kiss her career goodbye. Famous father or not, it wasn't a risk her agent was willing to take. At least in the beginning. Once Mel made a name for herself and had a few successful books under her belt, then all bets were off. Besides, her agent said, she didn't want Mel on the book circuit only being asked questions about her latest girlfriend or talking about the most recent vacation photos showing Mel canoodling. *Salacious* was being nice when it came to terms her agent used. *Pervert, sick,* and every other word that had been used to describe women who loved other women were thrown about in that meeting. Mel felt disgusted by the time it was all over, and she seriously questioned her place in the mystery world.

But it was her calling. For as long as she could remember, being a writer was all she wanted in life.

Her mother supported and encouraged Mel to pick up a pen and create the worlds she wanted to live in. Her agent had told her that if she wanted a shot at a book deal, she'd have to act accordingly. So, she'd punched down that part of her life and gave up on finding love.

Well, that part didn't last long, and now, years later, a reporter was snooping around. At some level, Mel felt betrayed. But by whom? She could guess, but Mel needed to try to stop the bleeding and keep her personal life personal. Her family, mainly her father, had no clue about her orientation. She knew how he felt about the LGBT community from his many diatribes at the supper table when they were kids. She'd sworn her mother to secrecy when her mom found out after she walked in on her and her best friend kissing.

Mel, the successful mystery author, didn't need to explain how she broke up the relationship of a top forensic scientist and her husband, or how she'd left her own girlfriend for said scientist, only to have it all fall to shit.

And that was clearly what was happening. Which was why she was here, back at home, in a town where people respected her privacy but never let her forget that they'd had a hand in growing her.

Mel reasoned that Pilar probably wouldn't be willing to stick it out for more than a day or two. Judging by her car alone, Pilar wasn't the kind of person who was used to going without luxury. And for all that Mel loved in this town, it was not a place that was rich in luxuries; the only available lodging around wasn't named "Hotel Quick" for nothing. The town and surrounding communities weren't rich in anything past cattle, stray cats, hens, and drinking buddies.

Everything else was hard earned and hard to

get. Mel turned the corner onto the main street, the sun casting a warm glow over the little haven. She had thought that the city was the right place to hide, but when push had come to shove, the country was where Mel knew she needed to go.

The thought of Pilar bringing big-city trouble out here to her was enough to leave Mel unsettled, a heavy weight settling at the base of her gut. There was a brief passing moment where she considered doing an interview just to make the woman go away, but it was a thought that Mel quickly brushed aside.

After all, the point of coming out here was so that she didn't have to deal with her problems. She'd left them back in the city along with the baggage that came with relationships. Bad breakups—everybody had them, and she wasn't exempt from the experience. She just didn't want to talk about it, or think about it. She just wanted to be left alone to sort out her life, and her old stomping grounds, where everyone treated her like a regular person, was just the place her soul needed to do that. At least that was what she kept telling herself every night.

So, no. Mel would not be doing an interview with Pilar Stein, or anyone else, about her relationship any time in the near, or far, future. She would just sit herself down at the diner with a milkshake, some fries, and wait until the nosy woman had gone elsewhere. Mike needed time to change out the tire anyway, so Mel figured she wasn't even out a whole lot, exactly.

What better treat was there to pass the time than a hand-churned milkshake, anyway?

None, that was for sure.

Mel spied the diner at the end of the street and set off for it, periodically looking over her shoulder for the journalist. She rarely made a lot of splurges lately. Running from the bad ending with Jill, plus a house that took up a lot of her time and money since there was always something that had to be bought or replaced, had kept her mind focused and her head down. Repairs, she had learned, were not cheap to do, and there seemed to be no end to things that had to be fixed up, changed up, replaced, and otherwise adjusted. She had second thoughts every time she was at the lumber yard or the hardware store and about to dump more on the money pit in the country and the big house she owned in the city that stayed somewhat empty. When things cooled down and she was no longer a wanted woman on the "where did she go?" circuit, she'd eventually venture back to the city. Besides, her assistant Emily still lived in the house and kept her apprised of schedules, tasks from her editor and publisher, and demands from her lawyer—which seemed to be endless.

Unfortunately, Mel had to hire a team of lawyers to clean up the mess with Jill, and then there was Carrie, her ex who had made it well known in their small circle of friends that she would ruin Mel in any way she could. That was enough to get her hired pit bulls to descend on her like a ton of bricks. Suits citing slander, libel, and defamation, plus the threat of keeping her knee-deep in legal bills, had cooled her stilettos—for now. To their credit, her legal counsel had found some very naughty details in Carrie's past and threatened to go to the media with them if she followed through with her threats of going public. While prostitution wasn't as shocking today as it might have been years ago, Mel was sure it would ruin any chances of resurrecting her failing TV career.

Mel wasn't thrilled with the walk, but she figured that the exercise was good for her. She hadn't had her once-usual strawberry milkshake in a while, and it sounded perfect. Besides, the diner was full of friendly faces, and she spread the word that her truck was in the shop just on the off chance that Pilar made it this far before she left.

The milkshake was just as tasty as Mel remembered, and she set up near the window so she would have a clear view of the roads and sidewalk leading up to the entrance, including eyes on a content Max, who had curled up in the sun next to a bowl of water the diner had outside for their canine customers.

There was no doubt the owner, Beth, would let Mel jump out the back door if she asked, needing to make a quick exit. Beth and Mel's mother had been close friends, and she was something like an aunt to Mel after having spent so much time around her growing up.

Much to Mel's pleasure, there was no sign of Pilar, and she could sit and enjoy her milkshake. A few sideways glances at her amused her. She wasn't sure if she would ever get used to people pointing and whispering, but she did her best to look unbothered, at least. While the townsfolk generally felt that run-of-the-mill celebrity scandals weren't worth their time, they were simply tickled that their small hamlet had produced not one but two famous authors, and they absolutely took pride in that fact. They also were fiercely protective of their own, so Mel saw their tittering around her as a fair trade for them circling the wagons when outsiders came looking to make trouble.

After Mel deemed that she had loitered long

enough, she made her way back to the garage to pick up her truck. No doubt Mike would have made changing her tires the priority if it meant he could get all the juicy gossip, especially after such an odd departure on Mel's end.

What was she going to tell him? Mel didn't want to spend the evening trying to rehash everything that had happened. She honestly wasn't at a point yet where she wanted to talk about it with anyone. And no offense to Mike, but a casual friend wasn't exactly who Mel wanted to be spilling her heart out to today.

❧❧❧❧

The man inside of the shop opened the rolling door after a moment. "Sorry, miss. Less it's an emergency, I'm turning in early for the day. We've got a nasty storm sweeping in soon, and I've got prep that needs to be done for it."

"This will just take a moment." Pilar shouldered her way into the garage and gave it a cursory look. It was the same as any other small-town building: a mash-up of pictures and old tin signs on the walls; ancient-looking gas cans set on display on a shelf system at the back of the room; and Mel's truck, sitting right there, hiked up on the jack. Bingo.

"Hi, I'm Pilar Stein, a reporter for the *Literary Times*, and I was hoping you could help me out."

"Never heard of the *Literary Times*, but if you got a busted a tire—"

"No—"

"Oh, bad radiator then?"

"Nope—"

"Well, unless you got a mechanical issue with

that Mercedes, I can't help you."

"Well—"

"Would you look at the time? I hate to rush you lady, but if I don't get home when supper is on the table, my wife will have my hide."

"I was hoping to ask you a couple of questions."

"Guess you'll have to come back tomorrow. Questions after five cost double time."

"Please, just one quick question."

"Best make it quick, then," Mike said.

"I'm looking for someone. Mel Crenshaw."

"Name sounds familiar. I think I might know her."

"I'm going to bet that you do," Pilar said. "Considering that's her truck right there."

Mike turned and gave the truck a slow look over. "So it is. Well, ain't that something? You a friend of hers?"

"Something like that. I'm trying to meet up with her. Do you have her contact info?"

Mike tilted his head back, looking up at the ceiling as if he had to give the question a hard mulling over. Finally, he announced, "Nope. Can't say that I've got it. We never really talked about that sort of thing. It was all business and the like."

Pilar drew in a sharp breath. It was obvious that the man was yanking her chain. A small town like this? Everyone knew everyone else. That was the charm and the cost of living somewhere with under five hundred people. And she got the impression that they were closing ranks.

The city was filled with ghosts and nameless faces, enormous buildings crammed with people hustling, conning, and plying their trade in a variety of ways to make a living. There were people everywhere who you would see once and then never pass again. The subway was constantly filled with changing faces and people trying to keep up with the day's busy pace, even stepping over the displaced people who littered the rail stations, bus stops, and homeless encampments that blotted the sidewalks.

Pilar was an exception, but only because her work required her to know people. And even then, it wasn't as though Pilar made a lot of friends when she did an exposé on someone. The journalist was just trying to make an honest living, and she tried to be as honest as possible. However, honesty wasn't often appreciated in the upper circles of the business world.

In fact, the homey sort of trust that probably meant you didn't lock your doors or close your windows on a sultry night seemed abundant out here in the country. It was so unusual to Pilar, in fact, that it made her oddly uncomfortable. She was used to people giving her tips and headlines within a few minutes of being chatted up. They often wanted their fifteen minutes of fame and would sell out their closest loved ones for it. She wasn't used to this whole dance that Mike seemed intent on doing. It was a challenge that Pilar hadn't been counting on, that was for sure.

Still, she tried to keep her voice level when she demanded, "Then why don't you look it up on her file for me? If it's not too much trouble. I could make sure that your garage is mentioned favorably in my cover story. The *Literary Times* is national, kind of a big deal."

That made the man laugh at her. It was a genuine, full-belly guffaw, the sort of laugh that was usually only heard at her house around the holidays when everyone had just a little too much wine or spirits before dinner. "Ma'am, I'm not sure your readers are the type to come all the way out here to get their oil changed, no offense." Mike shook his head and clucked his tongue. "Besides, out here in the country, we just trust people. She said that she'd be back for the truck later in the week. Last I saw, she had someone pick her up out front. I'm happy to let her know that someone's been asking after her, though. She might want you to leave a number or something."

"That's ridiculous. You must have some way of getting in touch with her."

"Now, I can tell that you're not from around here, but this ain't the city. She said that she'll be back this week to get the truck and pay me for my time, and I trust that she'll hold true to her word about it. I don't need to get in touch with her," Mike said.

It was infuriating. The harder Pilar tried to weasel more information out of him, the nicer the man became, and clearly just as unrelenting. No matter how Pilar tried to phrase it or what fake kindness she tried to use, the man wouldn't budge. Mike wasn't interested in how she offered to name-drop his garage in the profile, although it would do wonders for what was clearly a lackluster business. And he wasn't only not interested, the man laughed in her face. How did people function in hicksville?

The garage was empty save for Mel's truck and an old beat-up car. There was a lawn mower sitting off to the side of the garage, but it was hard to tell if that was in for work or just part of the odd, country decor of things.

Recognition in a widely circulated magazine would do the man well, but that did nothing to get him to change his mind.

And why?

Was Mel Crenshaw really so interested in her privacy that she had, what, bribed the locals? Just the thought of it was ridiculous. Pilar could offer this man far more than someone who was herself hiding out.

She ended up snapping at him. "Just call me if you hear from her." She tossed the card at the man, and both followed it as it hit his chest and then spun down to the dirty garage floor. "Oh, geez." She reached down to pick up the errant card and would have gone ass over teakettle if the man hadn't had unexpected quick reflexes. He scooped her up by her arm just as she almost face-planted onto the grimy floor.

"Thanks."

"Don't mention it." Mike took the card, looking at it like he wasn't entirely sure what the thing was, and Pilar made another frustrated sound in her throat before turning and storming back out to her car. It had been clear skies earlier, but a strong wind was kicking up, making the dark clouds building overhead twist about ominously. Pilar had no interest in getting stuck out here for any sort of large storm.

In all honesty, she had assumed that she would have finished here by now. Pilar had assumed that Mel wouldn't be practiced enough to keep herself under wraps out here; a false sense of security from living in a new place was normally enough to make the people Pilar chased slip up enough to get caught.

That hadn't been the case with Mel Crenshaw, though. The woman was a veritable ghost.

She slammed her door closed, grabbing up her phone and hitting the speed dial for her editor. Magdalena's voice snapped over the line. "What?"

She was a crusty, antiquated relic from a time when editors chain-smoked and were weighed down with makeup and costume jewelry. Magdalena's advancing years didn't slow her down. Their first meeting had been close to an exercise in torture, as Magdalena blew smoke in her face during the interview. In truth, the editor scared Pilar on some level—shoot, on every level—but she was determined to outlive the old bat, no matter what it took.

"Tell me you have something more for me to pursue."

"Pilar, this is your job. I've given you all the information that I've got. You're the investigative reporter. Investigate and report on something."

"I haven't even been able to find the damn woman."

"That sounds like a personal problem," Magdalena said. "A very personal problem. I'm going to be straight with you, Pilar. You've done good work for me over the years, but things have been dying down lately. Finding Mel Crenshaw and figuring out why she's all but disappeared is the only chance you have to stay relevant—and on my payroll."

The threat was thinly veiled, at best. Her words were often laced with editorial arsenic. Nevertheless, it sent a spike of anxiety through Pilar. She knew her job, maybe even her career, was resting on whether she could get this done, but it was still hard to hear.

Pilar did not like being threatened. She most certainly didn't enjoy thinking about being on her last chance. It wasn't her fault that the last exposé—a piece on a popular oil conglomerate—had gotten the magazine flack. Pilar hadn't even picked the man out to do an article on; that had been Magdalena. But it had made things complicated enough that Pilar was suddenly standing on rocky ground with the company, and even with the industry at large.

"I'm not saying that I've given up," Pilar said. That wasn't an option. There was no chance that she could give up—this was the only career that Pilar had ever wanted. She had devoted her life to becoming a competent journalist and working to build up a name for herself.

The thought of that changing now was…awful, really. It made her chest ache a bit, made her want to pick up a cigarette—several cigarettes—and start chain-smoking even though she kicked the habit almost three years back.

Magdalena said, "I have given you more leads than anyone else. Figure it out."

The line went dead.

Anyone else?

Did Magdalena have someone else working on the story?

That bitch.

Pilar held the phone for a moment, then tossed it onto the passenger seat next to her. She slammed both hands against the steering wheel. This was not how things were supposed to go. One woman shouldn't be so damned hard to find.

More determined than ever to catch Mel Crenshaw, and before the elusive *anyone else* did, she threw the car into drive and ripped out of the parking lot. There was more than one way to find someone. Pilar would just have to get creative.

If nothing else, Pilar was very good at being creative. It might turn out to be one of the toughest cases that she'd been on, but that meant nothing in the long run. Pilar could still work things out and get her career—and her life—back on track.

Magdalena's threat had only added to her growing foul mood. At the moment, it didn't seem like there would be a chance of Pilar getting her day back up to par, but she would just have to do…something.

Pilar would figure it out on the go. The town wasn't that big. Just because Mike had been on the reclusive side of things, that didn't mean everyone would. Pilar would bet that half the people in this town were aware of the fact that Mel Crenshaw had bought a house somewhere near here.

Someone was no doubt going to be loose-lipped enough to tell her about it. Pilar would find somewhere to get something to drink, do some footwork, and ask around that way.

Right. There was still a chance that she could do this. No, not a chance. Pilar refused to let anything come between her and finding Mel Crenshaw.

This profile *would* happen.

Pilar would make sure of it.

❧❧❧❧

Mike was waiting for Mel when she got to the shop. He had set up a lawn chair out front, had an open beer in one hand and the latest issue of an automobile magazine in the other. He was wearing sunglasses despite the weak evening sun lingering above the horizon, mostly, Mel assumed, so he had the chance to lower them down the bridge of his nose and look at her over the rim.

Mike had never lost his dramatic streak, that was for sure.

Mel gave him a sheepish wave. "Hey. Can I… pick up my truck?"

Slowly, Mike set his magazine down on the ground. He set the open beer can down on top of it before uncurling from his chair and giving a long stretch. She could hear his back crack from where she was standing; the sound made her flinch. She hated when people popped their joints around her. It always made her own bones feel stiff, but she couldn't ever bring herself to do it. It made her squeamish.

"You know, I closed an hour ago. I should make you come back tomorrow, like any other customer."

"You should," Mel said. "And I would deserve it, too. But damned if I don't feel like walking out to the house tonight."

"You're lucky I like you so much, Mel." Mike walked around to the front of the garage, bending down to roll up the aluminum door. "I didn't even lock up. Figured you'd be back around at some point today."

"She didn't give you too much trouble, did she?"

"Nope. Just an oddball if I've ever seen one. She's certainly not from around here, is she?"

"No, she's not." Mel knew it was rude not to offer any more information. She just hoped that Mike would take the late hour into account and let the social gab slide tonight.

Mike grabbed at his graying beard and tugged on it every few inches as he ran his hand down it, pulling it at the end. He was so country that most men could take lessons from him. He gave her a hard look and stood firmly in the center of the entranceway. Shaking his head, he clucked his tongue at her like one might at a horse that's not behaving. "All right.

Don't tell me. But I'll expect you to tell me what made you come home after all this time living in the big city and writin' them books I always see on the bestseller list, so you owe me, you hear? Especially if I'm going to run interference with the people showing up here asking after you."

"You're the best." Mel hurried in after him. "And I don't think that she'll be back here soon. She should be out of your hair for good, Mike."

Mike ran a hand through his hair. "Good. I don't need any added stress knocking this loose. I'm thinning early enough as is."

The truck was all ready to go. He grabbed the keys from behind the desk and tossed them to Mel as she handed over a wad of money. He never quoted her a price, and she was never sure if she over- or underpaid for the work. She suspected over, but Mike was a friend, and she always took care of her friends. She even gave him a hug for good measure, just to show how truly grateful she was. Still, as soon as the keys changed hands, Mel made her getaway. She wasn't in the mood for any more small talk.

"Come on, Max. Let's go home." Mel slammed the door and waved at Mike. "Catch you later, buddy."

He nodded and gave a quick wave before he dropped the garage door.

A glass of wine, alone on her porch. Now that sounded like heaven about now. Damn, she needed to stop by the grocery store before going home. Max had a little dog food, enough for one bowl for a dog that thought he was still growing. Maybe it was his sad eyes when he devoured the last of the kibble and started licking his bowl, or the way he lay down next to it afterward, his nose resting in the bowl, but she hated thinking that she wasn't feeding him enough. She needed a few things, and it didn't make sense to make a special trip back into town tomorrow. Once she got started working on the house she could go for hours, getting into the rhythm of physical activity. She'd been known to go late into the night before she realized the growling she heard wasn't Max but her own stomach. Often, breakfast had been the last time she had eaten on busy days. The reporter had thrown her off her routine, but she was in the past right now. Max was her immediate future, so she needed to make sure he was taken care of too.

❧❧❧❧

Mel pushed the limping shopping cart down the bread aisle. Scanning for her midnight snack—raisin bread—she scooped up two loaves, raised them above her head, and arced them into the cart.

"She shoots, she scores, and the crowd goes wild." Mel swung her arms back and forth, jumped up and down, and mimicked a roaring crowd.

She loved sports and missed her college days. In high school she was a three-sport athlete: volleyball in the fall, then basketball, and finally softball. The lesbian trifecta, Mel thought, shaking her head. Her basketball skills had earned her a scholarship to a Division III university. Her father had wanted her to forget sports and go to his alma mater. There was nothing she wanted less than to live in his shadow. So, she took the basketball scholarship, but later found out that the whole reason she was offered the scholarship was because of her father's high profile and the money that came with educating a Crenshaw kid. It solidified why she rarely saw court time, but the added bonus was the literature program with a focus on creative writing. Her mother had helped her see the bright side of everything, even the lack of playing time. At least her sister decided to bow to the pressure and go to their father's alma mater, lessening the focus on her. Clearly he'd been very convincing when he'd had "the talk" with Margo. It had taken the sting of disappointment off her shoulders, and thankfully Margo was good like that. She hadn't earned the nickname "Daddy's girl" by accident. It made her Lauden's favorite child, and he never let her and her siblings forget it. Their father constantly stressed that competition was healthy between the children, and that had bled over into their adult lives. While she had a loving rivalry with her brother and sisters, she always gravitated toward her mother.

Mel loved all of her siblings, but they were on different planets when it came to their parents. Her brother, the spitting image of their father, was the animal lover, following his passion to become a vet. Her sister Mallory loved attention and gossip, so she became a reporter. Her father considered this punching down but supported her anyway. However, Margo, who was always dissecting everything that was said in the house…she became a shrink. Her father would sit and debate with Margo for hours when she came home for the holidays. He said he was testing her critical thinking skills, but she suspected her father did nothing without his own hidden reasons.

Two moved away, wanting to experience all the world had to offer, and two stayed closer to their birthplace. Now, she made three in their hometown. Which reminded her—she owed her brother a catch-up phone call, but she'd been so busy and time wasn't on her side. As for Margo, she was the vinegar to her sister's oil, so she would wait to reach out. She missed her nieces and nephews, but a drama fest just wasn't in the cards right now. Besides, the holidays were just around the corner, and they would all get their fill of family, food, and arguments.

Her mother's kindness and actions echoed in her ear: "Be the bigger person, honey. You're better than that," or, "It takes so little to be kind, but being mean or evil takes a plan." God how she missed her mother.

Without thinking, she'd pushed her cart past the produce aisle, the selection sparsely populated with everyone having a garden. She stopped dead in her tracks, spotting Pilar Stein at the other end.

Shit, shit, shit.

Pilar was focused on something, so Mel slowly backed up her cart as she kept her gaze on her. Mel prayed she wouldn't see her and she could quietly leave the store.

Mel's cart hooked the display of chips on the end of the aisle and dislodged the endcap, sending bags of chips, dip, and wire rack everywhere.

"Fuck my life," Mel whispered, dropping her head and pushing her cart into the other aisle.

"Oh my, you okay, Dusty?"

"Oh, hey, Hazel. Yeah, good. Just thought I'd pick up a few things before that big storm hits and I remembered I forgot something." She motioned to the end cap and rolled her hands over and over. "Just hooked the buggy on the end and bam." She quietly slapped her hands together.

"Oh, that's okay, hun, happens more than you

can imagine." She bent down and started to gather up the bags of chips.

Mel kept an eye on Pilar at the other end of the store as she helped pick up the disaster she'd created.

"How's your dad?"

Mel shrugged. "I haven't seen him lately, but I hear he's doing good."

"Oh, I wanted to ask you when his next book is coming out. I just love that Navy SEAL series he has, reminds me of James when he was younger. All muscle-y and strong." She held her hand over her heart and patted her chest. "Grrrr, love me some men in uniform. Oh, not that your books aren't good. Gosh you sure have a gift with the way you turn a phrase, Dusty."

Mel blushed and waved the woman off. Her dad seemed to have that effect on lots of women. They practically threw themselves at him at his book signings, and on more than one occasion when she'd accompanied him on a few of his PR junkets, she'd seen a woman slip him a room key or a phone number. Her father would smile and dismiss them, and when Mel confronted him about the indecent proposals, he would say, *Part of the business, Melly. Part of the business.*

"I wish I knew, Hazel, but I'll tell him you're asking."

"Oh, gosh, Dusty, I would hate for you to bother him." She blushed.

"He loves it when readers ask, no problem." Mel stood and brushed her hands together. "Well, I think that's all of them."

"Thanks for the help. Most excitement I've had all day, 'cept did you hear George got a new heifer?

Yeah, his old gal finally stopped producing milk so he had to put her down."

"You mean, put her out to pasture?"

"Oh no, he went out and…" She made a gun with her fingers and put them between her eyes and pulled the trigger. "Put her down, said he couldn't afford to feed an extra head that wasn't producing."

"Gotcha." The idea that he had put the cow down wasn't a surprise to Mel. Country folks had a different way of thinking about their animals than those in the suburbs. They weren't pets, they were tools in the farmer's toolbox. Bottom lines were thin out here, and an extra mouth to feed was avoided at all costs.

Mel noticed Pilar was about half an aisle way from her, her cue to finish up and get out of Dodge.

"I'll see you up at the front, Hazel." Mel walked backward and two aisles over, then made her way to the cashier. Close calls were not her forte, and she was determined to avoid all contact with Pilar Stein.

Her anxiety ramped up as she unloaded her groceries onto the belt. "Come on, Hazel, come on."

Mel arched and looked down the aisle, trying to track down Pilar's location. She needed to ditch the persistent reporter before she discovered how close she had actually come to the subject of her story.

"Sorry, Mel. Someone needed my help." Hazel's welcoming smile took the edge off Mel's anxiety, but just as soon as she let her guard down, Pilar pushed her cart to the checkout. Pilar put a few items on the belt behind Mel's and focused on her phone.

Mel piped up as she quickly bagged her groceries and waved at Hazel. "I'll see you later, Hazel." Mel tossed a small nod toward the woman and raced out of the store.

Mel moved quicker as she heard Pilar ask Hazel about her.

❧ ❧ ❧ ❧

"You probably have your finger on the pulse of all the goings-on around here."

"Oh, I don't know about that, but I do hear all the good news that happens in town. Everyone comes in and we're just a friendly bunch. Small town and all."

"Would you say you know everyone in town?"

"Well, I've lived here all my life, so yeah. I've seen kids grow up, get married and have kids of their own, parents pass on, and a new crop of young people come and go."

"So, I guess you know Lauden Crenshaw. What do you think about the famous author who lives here?"

The woman blushed and waved her hand in front of her face, fanning herself. "Oh, I just love his books. He sure knows how to write some..." Hazel dipped her head close to Pilar, looked around furtively, and whispered, "Those steamy sex scenes...well..." She fanned herself again. "He's a very good writer, if you know what I mean."

Pilar played along. "I know what you mean. Seems talent runs in that family, doesn't it?"

"Oh, you mean Dusty? Yeah, she's a nut off the same oak tree."

"You know her pretty well?" Pilar said nonchalantly as she bagged the few items she'd purchased.

"Sure I know her. You just missed her. That was her in front of you."

"Mel—I mean, Dusty?" Pilar looked puzzled.

"Oh, yeah. That's what I call her. You probably know her as Melanie. But some of us call her Dusty."

Pilar looked out the huge plate glass window to see the taillights of the truck barreling out of the parking lot.

"Oh, I guess you didn't notice her 'cause you were on your phone." Hazel handed Pilar her change and smiled.

"I guess I didn't recognize her. She doesn't look anything like her pictures on the back of her books. How'd she get the Dusty nickname?"

Hazel leaned on the cash register and pulled a paper cup from the nook beside it, took a sip, and sighed. "Well, she did just get her hair cut. Went into the salon and told Cherie to chop it all off. Said she needed a change after moving back."

Pilar nodded and looked back over her shoulder, searching for which way the truck turned. Clearly, Hazel was the town gossip and nothing got past her. She'd know everyone and everything that happened in the small town. A resource more valuable than the internet. "So, how'd she get the name Dusty?"

"Oh, shoot. When Dusty was a kid, she'd hang around with my kids and they would go down to the creek and play all day. When they came home, I swear to God they looked like they'd taken a dirt bath, so I just nicknamed her Dusty and it stuck."

"What was she like as a kid?"

Hazel's smile flattened into a thin line, her brow furrowed, and she squinted at Pilar. Her body language was obvious, and Pilar prided herself on her ability to read people. Hazel was suspicious of all the questions.

"Who'd you say you were?"

"Oh, I'm a writer myself. My publisher wants

me to do a book on the Crenshaw dynasty and I'd love for you to be in the book as a resource, but only if you want. I mean if you don't mind me quoting you." Pilar knew she was lying to the woman about it being a book, but when some people found out you were a journalist versus a novelist, things went cold.

"You mean like people all over the world will read it, kinda book?" Hazel perked up.

"Oh, yeah, this will go nationwide." Pilar knew how to play on people's need for their fifteen minutes of fame, and it usually worked.

"Hmm." Hazel pursed her lips. "Well, I gotta close up."

The shift in the room was immediate, and Pilar knew the woman was freezing her out.

"Oh, sure." Pilar rooted around in her purse and pulled out a business card. "Well, if you wanna be part of the book, give me a call and we can set up an interview."

Hazel just nodded, grabbed her keys, and followed Pilar to the door. From the sound of the dead bolt being thrown and the buzz of the neon sign being turned off and the open sign being flipped over to the reaction from the mechanic earlier that day… it felt like Pilar was being sent a message. The city was closing ranks around their famous family, and outsiders weren't allowed inside.

It didn't matter. Pilar liked a challenge, and once she was on the trail it would take more than a few cold shoulders to shake her off it.

"Well, have a good night, Hazel," she said, waving to the woman staring at her from behind the locked door. "I'm sure I'll be seeing you again."

Chapter Four

Mel put as much distance between her and the market as fast as she could. Every time she looked in the rearview mirror she expected to see Pilar's Mercedes racing up behind her. Pilar wasn't classically striking but she was easy on the eyes, and as Mel closed hers, she inhaled and could almost smell her perfume. Dang, why couldn't Pilar just…*Just what, Mel?*

As Mel pulled up, she looked at the old ranch homestead. The house wasn't bad looking, but it certainly had seen better days, maybe a half a century ago. What she saw when she'd been shown the house was potential, what it could be restored to. On the outside, it wasn't too bad. The walls needed a good scrubbing and a fresh coat of white paint before the interior remodel started. The steps leading up the wooden front porch had been creaky and half were split or broken, so they had been replaced first. The traffic of moving in would mean a hospital bill if she hadn't dealt with them, so fixing them had been a straightforward decision.

The house had come with an old swing on the front porch, but the chains were so rusted that Mel wouldn't trust the thing to hold her weight. It creaked ominously in the late evening winds, and Mel decided it probably wasn't worth the trouble to fix, especially with her vision for a new layout. A revamped porch and deck would be the perfect place to survey her modest ranch land. The property didn't have as much acreage as some of the other places she had considered, but it was big enough for Mel and at least one or two ranch hands that would be hired in the spring. Mel envisioned pops of color on the deck as well. Potted flowers, plants, a firepit, and some comfortable deck chairs to replace the old swing would help provide more outdoor living space and fresh air in the spring and summer. All of that would have to wait since winter threatened to make an early appearance.

Besides, Mel wasn't ready to try to really get a farm going, yet. Her first foray into the fields with the dilapidated tractor that came with the house had only yielded a blown-out tire and a headache. She decided she needed to focus on her personal life, and she needed to get the house up and running first. The twenty-acre property would give her plenty to work with sometime down the line. There was enough room to put in a henhouse and a garden or two, and maybe a few grapevines. Perhaps she'd try her hand at winemaking and canning, too.

A gentlewoman farmer sounded appealing.

Mel dropped her groceries on the table and rummaged through them. She still couldn't believe how close she'd come to being discovered, bumping into Pilar at the store. Her only thought was to put as much distance between herself and the reporter. She'd tossed her bills on the conveyor and grabbed what she could and ran as fast as her legs would take her.

Max barked and nudged Mel's leg.

"What, buddy? You practically had a whole burger, you can't still be hungry."

Thinking about the list of chores that needed

to be done, she realized that she wasn't interested in tackling the outdoor stuff just yet anyway. Besides, there would be twice as much work outside as inside to get anything even close to being usable. A good mowing would be the best place to start, and she was decidedly lacking in the category of working knowledge of lawn care and lawn mowers. It had crossed her mind, of course, to ask Mike about loaning something out, but the man already did so much for her. She was sure he'd jump at the chance to spend more time together, but she didn't like the message it sent. A dusty road with a dead end and not a way forward.

What must the man think of her? Slamming his door down like that and then acting as if the police were on her tail. She was going to have to tell him more than the bare-bones story that she had shared so far. Mel wasn't ready for that yet, though. She didn't want to tell anyone. Even less so now that there was a reporter out and about, chasing after her like she was digging for gold, hoping to strike it rich. Mel knew her sudden disappearance was probably one of the hottest stories at the moment in the mystery world, which only added to her growing anxiety and did nothing to help her put the whole sordid affair behind her.

Irate, she breathed out and paused on the porch, leaning one shoulder against the wooden beam barely holding up the porch roof. It made her chest hurt a little bit, thinking about the day's events and how much work she had to do at the same time. Mike had been right, she realized. The hot water heater was important, but having a front porch that looked decent might be a close second, if only so coming home didn't send her into even worse of a funk.

What needed to be done out here? The front steps

were finished, so maybe removing the porch swing and shoring up the overhang. If it wasn't so close to the beginning of winter, Mel would be tempted to get a few potted plants to add a dash of color. Of course, it would be twice the work doing that now as she'd have to repeat it in the spring, but maybe getting one of those cute garden flags tacked up might do instead.

She really needed something that would brighten up the front of the house, she decided. Mel needed the place to at least feel like it wasn't threatening her every time she walked up to the front door. A set of wind chimes, maybe? They always had nice ones hanging about at the feed store, and the wind was certainly blowing hard enough that it would make quite a pleasant musical racket. That was it, then. The next chance she got, Mel was going to pick up a wind chime—maybe two of them—and hang them up out front.

The sky was ruddy out, darkening fast and with the threat of a storm about to blow in. Mike had been right about more than a few things today: it was going to be a hard, damned winter. It was obvious because the storm had blown in so fast. There was little doubt that it would break soon—and if it didn't, that would probably mean that a bigger storm would sweep in later on in the week.

She scanned the porch, the front lawn, and the massive trees that hung over the road coming onto the property. The temperature dropped a good thirty degrees at night, a sign winter was eking its way across the state. A bit of snowfall now would be preferred to a massive rainstorm in a couple of days. It was hard to tell just by the clouds which one she was going to have to deal with. Standing and squinting up at clouds just put her in an even deeper mood.

Damn.

It might not be so bad if she were living somewhere else, like back in the city. Originally, she had bought this house hoping that all the repairs it needed would keep her mind busy, and it had done so over the last month. But right now, it just made her miss the convenience of the city—and the oversized house she had tucked behind a gate that kept people like Pilar Stein away.

Warm, stale air hit Mel in the face as she stepped into the house. It still smelled musty, despite her best efforts at airing the place out during the day. "Great," she grumbled to herself. "This is absolutely the kick in the teeth I needed tonight. Come on, Max." She whistled.

The weather had been too bad to go out and leave the windows open, and it was too late in the evening to crack them now. Most were lacking screens, which meant the bugs would just come rushing in. The living room was mostly unpacked, a small miracle that had been a caffeine-driven first weekend in the country home, when she had thought a labor of love would mean a few quick scrub downs, a coat of paint, and some throw rugs here and there.

Mel spent the better part of her days in the living room as it was, so it made sense to spend her time fixing it up. The couch was worn, but she had a thick, heavy quilt that she'd thrown over the back which did a lot to hide the old threadbare cushions and make the place feel more like a home. The dog hair added character to the quilt, and if someone visiting didn't like dog hair, then they didn't need to visit. A new living room was being delivered in the next few weeks, so she'd make do until then. The living room was also the only place where she'd gotten anything hung up: a few pictures from events that she'd particularly enjoyed, and a couple of her hiking with her old dog Joshua that made her smile. The old boy was her constant companion until the day he died, just as her life was falling apart. God had a wicked sense of humor, and she wasn't sure how she'd made it through the other end of the dark tunnel, but she had. Sorta. Max had practically saved her life when she got him after her old boy died. He was the balm her soul needed and just the thing to help take her mind off the shit show that was her life at that time. The fact that she was still breathing was something, wasn't it?

Scanning as she entered the kitchen, she was met with the same disaster that it had been when she first moved in, though slightly cleaner. Only slightly, however, as she eyed the cobwebs in the room's corner with no small amount of distaste. She knew this would be the next room to tackle.

She sat her lone bag of groceries down on the kitchen counter, braced one arm against it, and tried to picture what the place would look like once it was up and running right. The curtains still needed to be replaced. Walls needed a coat of paint. The table was still piled full of boxes and newspapers from Mel's initial move-in. She had to scrub out all the cabinets before any of her dishes could be unpacked, and it was taking longer than she had expected.

She'd had a lot of bowls of cereal for dinner over the last few days and was not looking forward to having another. She should have invested in something a little more fulfilling to replace her sugary downfall. Maybe oatmeal or a TV dinner would be easy enough to make and help with her limited culinary experience. She'd traded knives and an apron for a writing pad and typewriter in her youth. Home Ec classes were the only Fs on her transcript, while journalism and yearbook made her heart sing.

Mel grabbed a piece of paper and a pen, jotting down oatmeal, TV dinners, and hot chocolate, and used an old apple-shaped magnet to slap the list to the front of the fridge. There. That was at least the start of being more organized and put together, although it unfortunately didn't help her situation tonight. She wondered if she should have had two burgers, since Max had eaten hers, or if the fries and milkshake from the diner would have to see her through the night. If she got really starving, she'd break out the cheese and crackers tucked away for safekeeping in an emergency. And, of course, there was the raisin bread.

She briefly thought about going back to town. But honestly, by the time she even made it to town, the grocery store would be closed for the night. So, that was actually only half a solution. Her stomach gave an angry grumble, loudly stating that it was not in the mood to be put off and ignored no matter how much Mel didn't want to find anything to cook.

If she were still in the city, she would have been able to just pour a glass of wine, call up a pizza, rent a movie, and enjoy the night. But this was the country, and that wasn't an option. Thinking about it just made Mel's mood that much worse.

Then again, if this were the city and she were in her house, she could get a hot shower tonight.

Instead, she still had the blown-out hot water heater to deal with. Mel knew she would find instructional videos online to fix it, but it would not be easy. Never say never was her motto. If push came to shove, she'd worked through enough repairs using YouTube University that she was pretty confident that she'd have hot water before she missed it.

She made quick work of putting her groceries up, treating them more roughly than the poor head of spinach or bag of flour deserved. Her stomach growled again and demanded attention, yet nothing interested her. Spying a bag of chocolate-covered peanuts, she briefly wondered if maybe chocolate would lift her mood…no, chocolate and wine would definitely lift her mood. She'd deliberately left a couple of cases of her private reserve stacked on the kitchen floor for easy access.

In the end, she actually wanted to eat something a little more substantial. The chocolate and wine she would save for the end of the night. She cracked two eggs into a bowl from the table, whisked them briefly, and shoved it into the microwave. It was not exactly the start of a tasty omelet, but at least it would be warm in her stomach.

Not wanting to completely torture herself with the meal, Mel did search out the salt, pepper, and ketchup, which she applied to the eggs in liberal amounts once it was done cooking. Mel fished out her toaster and tossed in two slices of bread. Two minutes later she slid the egg mixture onto the unbuttered toast. She wasn't one to stand on formality, so she did what she did most nights and promptly ate it while standing over the sink to catch the crumbs.

This was not the lowest point she had ever had, but Mel was very much aware that it wasn't her highest point, either. She washed up the bowl when she was done eating, knowing that it would just sour her morning if she left it lying around overnight. Not to mention that the thought of any four- or eight-legged creatures venturing inside on a scouting mission for food didn't make her particularly happy.

When it was all done and dusted, she decided she might as well brave the cold shower and get it over with, if only so she had an excuse to change into soft pajamas and curl up on the couch for the rest of the evening in front of the fireplace. She was only halfway into the living room when a sudden shrill note of music cut through the otherwise heavy silence of the house.

Her phone ringing startled her so badly that she jumped. Mel hurried to answer it.

"Hey, this is Andy, with Handy Andy's."

"Oh. Thanks. I was hoping I would hear from you today." Mel made her way into the living room, sinking down into the worn recliner. "Say, are you on local time?"

There was a running joke in town that there was a special local time, meaning you could expect the contractor to be an hour late, or maybe not even show up at all. You'd instead get a phone call an hour later explaining that some "crisis" popped up and they wouldn't be there that day.

It drove Mel crazy. That was something that she had never noticed when she was growing up out here. Now, it seemed to be everyone's sole goal to put her as off schedule in her renovation timeline as possible.

The man on the other end chuckled. "Depends on the day. Now, you wanted me to come by and give you some quotes, right?"

"That would be great. I'm trying to fix up an old farmhouse I just purchased. You know the O'Donnell place? I've done some of the simple stuff on my own, fixing the stairs and all that. But I don't trust myself up on the ladder, or messing with wires."

"No problem." Andy had a deep drawl that marked him as not originally being from the region. It made for a good phone voice, though.

They spoke a few minutes longer, with Mel giving Andy a laundry list of chores and setting a time for Andy to come by and give a quote, and then Mel found herself once more in silence as she hung up the phone.

Mel trotted upstairs, careful of the ones that creaked, and into her room. Unlike the living room, it was mostly in a state of disarray. This room required little in the way of repairs, though she had used duct tape and cardboard to fix a crack in one of the windows. It was, however, currently the place where Mel rooted through all the unpacked boxes in search of "the one thing she needed" and then promptly left the mess to be cleaned up another time. The result was a bed covered in papers and clothing, with just enough room for a Mel-sized body to stretch out on the mattress. This was why she had slept on the couch downstairs more often than not since she moved in.

Mel was very much aware of the fact that she was just making things more complicated for herself by letting the clutter pile up, but she couldn't seem to help it. Getting the bedroom cleaned up and looking nice felt like some sort of finality, the last nail in the coffin of her latest mistake. But she'd soon make the bedroom her personal refuge as she'd done in every house she'd lived in, this one with no ghosts of Jill.

She walked next door to her office, the neatest room in the whole house. She'd purposely kept it immaculately tidy so she would have no distractions while working on the new book. When she got around to working on it, that is.

She had only just started to fiddle with the computer when her phone rang again. This time, it was Emily McMillan's number displayed on the screen. Her assistant had impeccable timing.

Mel took a deep breath before she answered. "Hey, Emily. Tell me this is just a friendly chat to see how I'm doing."

"You know I wish I could. No, the chief wanted me to touch base with you."

"Right. About the new novel."

"Bingo."

Mel's lips thinned out. She knew she had to get the book done—she had put a lot of time and effort into writing the serial killer series. She just didn't think that she could handle dealing with that tonight.

The thought of having to go through the novel, which she'd started while in her relationship, made her stomach knot up. It was a trip down memory lane she wasn't ready to take when she was already having an awful night, and it didn't help that she hadn't opened the wine yet.

"I'll get it done, don't worry. Tell Torrance to lay off the guilt and cut me some slack. I'm almost done with the damn thing." A little white lie never hurt anyone, and Mel would get to it, eventually. Besides, she *would* get it done. It just probably would not be tonight. It probably wouldn't be tomorrow, either. Over the month, maybe? That seemed far enough away that Mel could get her shit together and make certain that the whole situation with Pilar Stein was settled and done.

"Good," Emily said. "Thanks, Mel. That means a lot. I know things are rough right now, but—okay, wait, no, before you hang up. I've had two calls."

"For me or about me?"

"Both. Carrie called. She's demanding to talk with you."

Mel wanted to deal with her pre-Jill psycho ex even less than she wanted to dive into the novel she was working on.

Mel made an unhappy sound. "Just refer her to the lawyer. I shouldn't have any direct contact with her. Tell me that the other one was good news?"

"I mean, it was news, at least," Emily said.

"That's not reassuring."

"It was a journalist. Pilar Stein. She's been calling pretty often since you left, wanting an interview."

"Met her already." Mel was unable to keep the unhappiness about it out of her voice. "I don't like her, and I'm not looking at talking to her about anything."

"Noted."

"I mean it, Emily. I don't want you to tell her where I live, no matter what."

"Noted," Emily said again, with a bit more force behind the answer. And then, "How are you holding up, Mel? For real? How is Max adjusting?"

"Max is good. He loves the country."

"Great. How are you, though?"

Wanting to change the subject before it turned into a shrink visit, Mel stood and walked back to her bedroom, then asked, "Hey, any news on the movie deal?"

Mel's book series had been optioned by a huge streaming service, and the deal was looking like it was going to net her money along the lines of the latest book sensation from a rival author called *Lover Lost Lover*. The prospects were mind-numbing, but it was fun to think about all of the things that could come from her book. *LLL* had movie posters, music, apparel, coffee mugs—even its own wine. All those and more could be hers as well, all she had to do was sign on the dotted line. There was talk of a mystery game spinning off from her book.

"I heard from Torrance today that they want the option to make a clothing line…T-shirts mostly, but heck, Mel, it could be worth tons of cash on top of all of the other stuff. Exciting, huh?"

It was, but Mel also wanted to get her life back to normal. She needed to free herself from as much distraction as possible until she had her head back on right.

"Mel?"

Mel looked around her bedroom and heaved a sigh before dropping backward onto the one clear sliver of the bed. The old mattress creaked under her weight, slight as it might have been. "I'm here. I'm here, and I'm working through things."

"Something I can do? Outside of keeping the dogs at bay, I mean."

"Magically teach me how to fix a hot water tank."

Emily hissed on the other end of the line. "Ouch."

"Yeah. You're telling me."

"Heat a pot on the stove."

"What?"

"Or in the microwave. Heat enough water you can wash up with. I've done it a few times, when I was waiting for the landlord to fix things. It's not great, but it'll make you feel clean again. Trust me. That helps."

A half smile flitted across Mel's face. "That's a good idea, Em. Thanks."

They talked for a little longer, mostly about what Emily had been up to, and then Mel found herself homesick for the city. It was going to take time to adjust to her new place and life, but at least this time her chest didn't hurt quite so much.

Mel and Emily might have met through work, but there was no way to deny that Emily was the closest thing to a best friend she had. They had been through a lot of shit together. Out of everyone, Emily knew most of the full story behind Mel and Jill's rough breakup, and Mel's move out to the country.

Not that Emily approved. She called it running from problems, which wasn't what Mel was doing.

It wasn't.

She was just handling things in her own way.

Remembering what she had with Jill came very close to shattering the good mood that Emily's talk had brought about. Mel was quick to shove it aside, groaning as she pulled herself up off the bed. She shook her head, grabbed her pajamas, and made her way back downstairs.

She used Emily's instructions for heating water, feeling a little embarrassed that she hadn't come up with the obvious solution on her own. Then, when she was clean and changed, she went out to settle down in front of the fireplace and watch every bad episode of the newest serial killer series. She would criticize every mistake, obvious clues to guide the viewer to the ultimate conclusion, and hope it was boring enough to help her fall asleep.

Without thinking, Mel grabbed the remote on

the table and pushed the button, expecting it to come to life.

"Fucking idiot. Seriously, you'd think I'd remember to call," Mel said, tossing the controller back on the table. Unfortunately, the TV wasn't hooked up yet, so she'd have to settle with watching something she'd saved to her tablet.

"Come on, Max. Bed?" Mel patted the sofa and made room for Max. It was going to be another long night.

She leaned her head back against the couch and sighed. Absently she stroked Max's head and smiled down at him as he laid his head on her thigh. Her mind raced with the day's events, especially the reporter. It'd been a while since she'd let herself think about a woman, and now suddenly all she could think about was Pilar Stein.

Why was she here, in her hometown, looking for Mel? Or maybe she was here to talk to her father.

This line of thought wouldn't get her anywhere. She suspected she would find out soon enough if Pilar was the journalist she'd read about. No, Mel was sure she would find the woman on her doorstep soon enough.

She flicked her wrist and brought up the movie she'd dozed off watching the night before. While it wouldn't win any awards, it was enough to take her mind off things and hopefully quiet her racing thoughts.

"Hello, Mel." A soft voice whispered in her ear. Her head was fuzzy, but she recognized the voice.

"What are you doing here?" Mel tried to rub her eyes, but her arms were pinned, Pilar's weight holding her down. Her lips hovered just above Mel's, taunting her. Her warm breath on Mel's neck sent a tingle throughout her body.

"I wanted to talk to you about fucking me..."

Mel jumped when Max barked, jostling her out of sleep and the best dream she'd had in ages.

Chapter Five

Pilar sat in front of the motel where she'd rented a room for the night. It was the only motel the town had to offer. Plus, it remarkably had cell service. That was the only perk the dilapidated shelter seemed to offer.

How could she have left the grocery story on a wild goose chase hoping to catch the receding truck's taillights? Shaking her head, she'd missed the obvious signs when she'd stopped to talk to the man—at least she had thought it was a man—fixing the flat tire. Some investigative reporter she was. How was she going to explain this to her editor?

The motel itself was technically twenty minutes outside of the town proper, on a stretch of flat empty land that was as barren as the eye could see, with a view a little too close to the highway than it probably should be. It was a single-floor building, flat and narrow, and looked like it might have come out of every B-grade horror movie that Pilar had seen over the years.

Not that the man working the counter was skeevy. On the contrary, he was polite enough, and seemed to lack any pervy qualities motel managers had in those movies. A good thing. Pilar wanted to do an article on Mel Crenshaw, not accidentally discover the next human trafficking ring or small-town murder operation out in the middle of the state.

Most of the rooms were dark as she unloaded the car. Pilar hoisted both of her bags with her, not wanting to make a trip back out to the parking lot to get them. Despite the fact that the lot was well lit and fairly empty, every sound, from the soda vending machine starting up to the ice machine shifting the melting cubes, was unnerving.

Pilar was used to operating under the rules that being in the city provided. It was strange trying to figure out how they might carry over to a new locale. Until today, Pilar had been certain that the movies always exaggerated how different life was between the city and the country.

Now it was clear they might not have been over-the-top enough.

Pilar's room was dead center in the building. She might have preferred one at the very end of the stretched-out building so there wasn't an adjoining room on either side of her, but it lacked a parking spot in front of it—a preference she wasn't willing to budge on. The room was small and dark, with a single full-sized bed and sheets that looked more than a little stained. If it hadn't been for the noxious bleach odor, she would have guessed that they were dirtier. She unloaded her bags into the corner of the room, set her laptop bag on the desk, then slipped her small bag of groceries onto the bed. Suddenly nothing she purchased looked appealing.

Pilar looked around for a sheet of delivery menus that could normally be found on hotel side tables but realized that option wasn't actually available.

"Really?" Pilar grumbled to herself, unhappily rooting through her purse in search of loose coins. She liked her salads, her steaks, and her occasional splurge on frozen yogurt. Still, hungry was hungry, and Pilar got *nasty* when she was feeling hungry. *Watch out, Melanie Crenshaw,* was all she could think as she pulled out her phone. The only reason she was sitting on a broken-down bed and foraging through her purse for change was because of that woman. Not to mention that she found it almost impossible to work when her mind was occupied by the empty state of her stomach. With no other options, Pilar raided the nearby vending machine for honey buns and chips—she had the sweet and salty covered—and now on to the soda machine. She was going to have so much making up to do when she returned to the city. One extra Zumba class was *not* going to be enough to account for all the extra carbs and sugars that she was about to shovel into her mouth.

No sooner had she gotten back to the room than her phone rang. Certain that it was Magdalena calling again, Pilar opened the phone without checking the number, snapping, "What?"

It wasn't Magdalena.

Randy Harlin's voice filtered over the line. "Well, that's one way to talk to me, I guess."

Pilar had the decency to cringe, at least. Randy was the PI that she had hired to help dig up dirt on Mel Crenshaw. He had come highly recommended, but so far he wasn't exactly panning out.

"Sorry," she said. "It's late and I'm starving. Tell me you've got something good."

"Depends on your definition of good. I've got something."

"Is it an address?"

"Sort of."

"Are we going to play twenty questions, or are

you going to tell me?"

Randy laughed. "I've got it on good authority Mel Crenshaw is a lesbian."

The words settled like a deflated balloon. "Duh. Tell me something I don't already suspect."

"It's just a rumor. I don't have any hard proof yet, but it's a rumor I think will check out. Word is that she left her girlfriend for the very smart and very married Jill Steele, a bigwig in law enforcement."

"The coroner?"

"Forensic scientist. Apparently, they were pretty hot and heavy until Jill's husband found out about the affair. Looks like Melanie turned tail and ran home to avoid a scandal."

"Anything else?"

"An address," Randy said. "Not hers, but her father's. No one would talk to me about him. He's like persona non grata. Something's going on there. No idea what it is, but my nose tells me there's something there. I'm sure of it."

Randy read off the address. Pilar jotted it down on the yellow sticky pad that the motel left on her bedside table. She stared at the numbers, punching them into the map app, and the location jumped out at her. Amazing, it was just a few miles away from the motel.

Pilar was like a dog with a bone. She never stopped until she had all the details, and this one could make her profile explosive.

"Good...great. That's great. That's a big start. You'll keep looking?"

"I'll keep looking," Randy said. They hung up a moment later, leaving Pilar alone in the quiet motel room once more, only this time nothing about it felt daunting. It was too late to do anything now, so she grabbed her laptop, sat back against the headboard, and typed the headline to her story: *Melanie Crenshaw—Reclusive Lesbian Novelist…*Backspacing, she started again. *Successful author Lauden Crenshaw…*

Pilar knew there was more to the woman than just another award-winning author who suddenly moved to the country for her health. But what was it? And now the father added another layer to her investigation. Maybe she could smoke Melanie Crenshaw out, if she could just figure out what secrets the Crenshaw family was hiding.

It would be tricky, but it was nothing like putting together an exposé on an acclaimed killer, or someone with enough money and power under their hand to leave smears in Pilar's personal life and career.

Mel Crenshaw was just…someone that the people found interesting. An adored novelist who valued her privacy, but her fans wanted to know more. A challenge, but not an endgame. So why did it feel so different?

Pilar didn't want to think about it. She wished she had wine, or something tastier than a honey bun. The slick sweet of the treat stuck to the roof of her mouth and caked into her teeth. She redoubled her efforts to find a channel that wasn't so static riddled it couldn't be watched.

Eventually, she settled for some late-night quiz show. Pilar settled in cross-legged on her bed and set to polish off the honey buns. This was the bombshell she could use to get doors to open.

Tomorrow, she would make a run out to speak to Lauden Crenshaw. With any luck, he would spill the beans on his daughter. She could even do it without pushing if she played her cards right. Tell him she was there for *his* interview. All Pilar had to do was appeal to his ego, hint that the profile was on Lauden himself, and he would eat it up. She knew people, and she knew how ego played in women and men who liked power, privilege, and fame—especially if they had it before and now craved it again.

Pilar would have him eating of her hands in a matter of minutes. Feeling more confident in herself, Pilar could settle in for the rest of the night, able to relax without worrying about the lede to her story. It was old hat for her, a trade secret, using people close to the *genuine* interest of the subject to gather intel. The people in town might not have had much to say about Melanie Crenshaw, but Pilar had been around enough authors, defunct and otherwise, to know that they loved talking about themselves, their accomplishments, and whatever tragedies they felt made their life unique.

Everyone had a story. It just came down to which one was interesting enough to be paraded in the public eye, and whoever handled their *story* the best once it was on display for all the world to see was the winner. But that wasn't Pilar's problem. Mel Crenshaw's decision to run away from a prestigious career as a writer and move out of the city just screamed that she was following in her father's pattern of poor decisions.

The fact that Lauden Crenshaw had been just as famous an author as his daughter nearly two decades earlier—*had been* being the operative words—was a contrast to good decisions made earlier in both their careers. Pilar could turn that into a story just as easily, to be revisited later. More important, though, was the fact that Pilar knew precisely how to take someone's decisions and use them to tease open private thoughts and internal reflections that led to a good story. No, a great story.

This was going to be easy.

She finished her honey buns, started pounding out an outline for her story, and finally went to bed, already thinking about what questions she would ask him in the morning. She was so giddy at the new outlook that she was going to have a tough time sleeping.

❧ ❧ ❧ ❧

Pilar left the motel almost before the sun had fully risen. It made the sad state of the parking lot and motel even more obvious. In the light of day, it was a worn-down thing and somewhere she never would have stayed normally. A faded flock of plastic pink flamingos was wedged into the ground just beneath the sign announcing its age, more than beckoning the traveler to enjoy its hospitality.

Pilar moved into the front lobby, where a continental breakfast comprised of cellophane-wrapped pastries, the kind you found at the local bulk warehouse, lined the folding table. The promise of something *continental* turned out to be a lie, or at least a stretching of the truth. There was a single coffee pot sitting on a wooden table just inside of the room, and another basket filled with prepackaged muffins. A wooden bowl half filled with apples and partially green bananas gave the only healthy option, as far as Pilar was concerned.

Did no one in the country understand what a carb was? Maybe they just all had the most ridiculous metabolisms known to man? The woman currently sitting behind the front desk looked just shy of being skin and bones, despite the healthy glow of the skin and the nicely toned muscles of her arms. Pilar had noticed that it had been the norm so far, the tan and the muscles and the lack of fat on anyone that wasn't over sixty. Clearly, the receptionist wasn't eating the continental breakfast, and if she did, it probably made a fast track out the way it had entered. Country life seemed to build more than just character, Pilar thought, passing on the pastries. Grudgingly, she made herself a cup of too-strong coffee, adding in as many of the little pods of half-and-half as she could feasibly justify using, and then another two just for good measure.

After rooting around through the fruit bowl, she came away with a banana and justified that decision by deciding that the guilt trip of the pastry would play on her mind all day. Technically, it was still a healthy choice, and a cheap one at that. The banana was rock hard in her mouth, but she was hungry enough to eat it with only minimal mental complaints.

She put the address into her map app for Lauden Crenshaw's place. The woman behind the counter had tried to be helpful but her blabbering only made her head spin, so she thanked her for the help and headed out. On her way out, Pilar stopped at the table and considered picking up another banana for the road but decided the bellyache she was going to have after the first wasn't worth the effort. She reached down, her hand hovering over the apple, but she thought better of it as well. Even the apples weren't worth the risk.

The parking lot was just as empty. Even with

the sun peeking out in the sky, a certain unmistakable dread had settled over the countryside. There was a heavy mist hanging just above the ground. It was rolling through the fields that she passed by, in some spots so heavy that it appeared like the cattle and horses within the fences were floating on nothing. Unfortunately, it made her drive time that much slower. Pilar wasn't used to the bending roads that wove between the fields, and she certainly wasn't used to all this fog.

It was strange being so far away from the city. The streets would be full of passing cars adding to the traffic; people hustling on the sidewalk; briefcases, umbrellas, and business attire accented with the occasional jogging suit racing past people. It felt odd being out in the country, where there was basically nothing around. The roads were desolate. Was it possible to feel claustrophobic when you were surrounded by nothing? It felt as though the emptiness could crush her if she dawdled long enough. Not for the first time, Pilar found herself missing her loft apartment and the luxuries within. She had a handful of fish and a neighbor that was fairly trustworthy when it came to keeping them fed, but Pilar wanted her shower with its dual massaging heads, and she wanted to just fall onto her fluffy mattress and memory foam pillow.

She hated going out of the city to chase down leads, and found a new, special hatred in coming out to this particularly small town. Pilar would have to make sure that she left the farm early enough that she could stop by a grocery store and get something that wasn't a honey bun or a cheap muffin for dinner. At this point, even a microwave TV dinner would be a better choice and make her feel a little less homesick.

Ugh. Pilar hated that word.

She should have been more than capable of leaving home for any amount of time. She was a grown woman, for God's sake, and shouldn't be so attached to a place that made her chest ache when she wasn't there. At least, that used to be the case…before. Before "Mr. Clean," the subject of her Pulitzer-Prize-winning exposé on money laundering and the drug cartels, had taken umbrage with the direction of her interview. He'd made his desire for her to drop the story clear through his fists—and his knife. Now, it took all the energy she had to do any sort of travel, to leave her cocoon of comfort.

Pilar shook her head to stop thinking about her anxiety and focused on the road, the destination, and the task ahead. The sun had finally started to burn away some of the fog. The only thing it didn't do was burn away the thick layer of clouds that hung in the sky, darker and heavier than they had been the day before. Huge, thick gray clouds that threatened impending doom. At least, that was the way she felt.

Great. Stuck in the country with an approaching storm. That was not how Pilar wanted to spend her time, dodging cow pies and mud puddles. Besides, she didn't have a raincoat, rubber boots, or an umbrella. Nothing. She would just have to make sure that she had enough detail to put in the profile so she could leave town and get back to the city before the storm fully broke and unleashed what she could only assume would be one of those gully washers. That's what they called it out here in the sticks, wasn't it?

Pilar followed the map directions on her phone for Lauden Crenshaw's place, astonished that the app stayed connected all the way to her destination. Asphalt led to gravel roads that eventually turned into dirt. She couldn't miss the enormous house that Lauden Crenshaw lived in if she tried. A security box stood sentry at a huge metal gate, meant to keep out, what? Cows?

Pulling up closer, she pressed a button on the call box.

"Can I help you?"

"Hi, I'm here to speak with Mr. Crenshaw."

"And you would be?" A heavy, gravelly voice that had smoked a pack too many cigarettes asked.

"I'm Pilar Stein. I'm a freelance journalist doing a piece on Mr. Crenshaw, and I know this is a little unorthodox, but I was hoping he would see me."

"A piece of what?"

"A magazine piece."

"What magazine?"

"Well, if I meet my deadline, the *Literary Times*."

"That fucking rag."

Pilar sighed. This was going to be more difficult than she thought. Her assessment of appealing to his ego might not work if he hated the magazine.

"Is this Mr. Crenshaw?"

"It is."

"Great. Mr. Crenshaw, I think you have a great story that needs to be told. You have been successful and then your daughter has followed in your footsteps. I'm interested in how you became a writer and how you raised a daughter who took the same path."

It was silent. Dang, she'd blown her opportunity to weasel her way into his good graces and any hope of helping her with her actual story on Melanie Crenshaw.

Without another word, the buzzer signaled the gate's impending opening.

"Thank you," she shouted into the box.

The long dirt road deposited her right in front of the monstrosity of a house. The sound of dogs barking filled the air. She lingered in the car for a long while, putting the soft top of the Mercedes up and making sure that none of the dogs barking planned on coming outside and nipping at her legs, before getting up and making her way to the front porch.

While the house was huge, it had seen better days. A little downtrodden, but only in the way old people's homes tended to be when they lost interest or mobility and didn't want to hire help to keep up a place this size. Pilar had interviewed a lot of parents, uncles, aunts, and grandparents over the years. It was in the extras—the sun-faded cushions put out on the little rocking chair on the front porch, the way that there were still flowers growing in the garden but the beds weren't as well weeded as they could be, and the general fact that there appeared to be a lot of property that wasn't currently in use—that Pilar recognized a house that had outgrown its owner.

She took in the surrounding landscape as she walked up onto the front porch. An old, rusted-out truck parked just to the side of the porch wasn't a usual tell, but Pilar supposed it was just another eccentricity that came with being in the country. It added to the cowboy feel she was expecting when she imagined Lauden Crenshaw. Actually, the truck was pretty similar to the one she'd seen Melanie Crenshaw changing a tire on. Yep, the acorn didn't fall far from the tree, did it?

Pilar pulled out her cell phone and snapped

a few photos of the house, the garden, and the old pickup truck. She preferred sleek, modern cars that still had that new car smell. Still, that could absolutely serve to keep the conversation going with Lauden, and so Pilar filed the information away for later use. A good reporter always had backup plans for casual chitchat, and if the subject of being an author didn't pan out, this could be just as good a way to keep her in the house and keep the man talking. Then she noticed the bright red sports car sitting on the other side of the porch.

Aw, there was the man she suspected lived in the house. A fire-engine red Lamborghini sat next to a huge black pickup truck that looked like she'd need a stepladder to get into. Why did people jack them up like that?

A knock on the door and a brief wait later had Lauden standing in front of her on the other side of an ornate screen door. He was an older man, long and lanky, wearing jeans, cowboy boots, and a button-down shirt. In the center of the man was the biggest silver belt buckle she'd ever seen. He looked her up and down and then shook his head like he couldn't quite understand what she was doing on his front porch. Finally, he asked, "You lost, ma'am?" He laughed after the question and held the screen door open for her to enter.

"No. I was actually hoping to talk to you," Pilar said. She gestured over her shoulder. "I'm doing a profile on authors, and I wanted you to be the starring piece."

She expected Lauden's entire face to light up, but his gaze was more like a granite relief. He tossed her a look that almost bordered on unenthusiastic. A shock of white hair sliced through the brown locks, giving him a dramatic look for an older man.

"Why would you want to talk to me?" He swept his hand wide, ushering her in. "Why don't you come in? I was just about to put coffee on. Want some?"

"That sounds delightful," Pilar lied. If it was anything like the motel sludge, she was sure she'd be cursing the man later in the day when she was hugging the porcelain goddess. Did no one know how to make a decent cup of coffee?

She followed the man into the house, looking keenly for anything that might give her a better glimpse into the childhood of Mel Crenshaw. Oddly enough, there didn't appear to be a single picture of the young woman in the home. Photos of Lauden Crenshaw with literary and political giants lined the walls. Awards dotted the bookshelves, acting as bookends for hard copies of his books. Covers in frames also ran up the walls to the high ceilings of the house. It was clear he had been a prolific writer. The house bore the same shades of wear as the front porch and the yard. At some point, it was no doubt an incredible place to live: the huge staircase that led to who knows where, the leather sofas that had cow hides draped over their backs. A rocking rooster sat under a window. Pilar wondered if it ever saw action. She knew Melanie Crenshaw had siblings, but no evidence of them, like Melanie, was in the house. There was a sizable collection of writing paraphernalia lining the mantel above the fireplace, but they had not been cleaned in a long while.

This was the home of an older man who lived by himself and maybe didn't get many visitors. Pilar wondered if Lauden was on the OCD spectrum.

Everything was in its place, like feng shui on steroids. Eccentric was the word that came to mind, but being organized wasn't necessarily eccentric, was it?

Pilar was led into the kitchen, which wasn't much better. The rooster decor appeared to be everywhere, some of it old and worn, and others bright. Many of them were truly, in her opinion, just the most hideous things that she had ever seen in her life. Pilar wondered if the cocks were a reference to something she didn't understand.

She wasn't planning to comment on them, but then she let it slip.

"Nice roosters."

It earned her an amiable smile from Lauden, who said, "My wife started the collection when she first moved in here, and I suppose I've just kept it going. Some of my friends give them to me over holidays, but mostly I pick them up myself. The only good to ever come out of the internet, if you ask me, is the ability to shop through it."

"I can think of a lot of people who consider that a phallic—I mean fallacy," Pilar said, directly referencing herself. Whenever she was particularly upset about something or overly intoxicated, she had the horrible habit of getting online and buying things she did not, under any circumstance, need to own. For example, she had a pair of dolls that were lovingly knitted, which she had purchased for some unfathomable reason and currently kept hidden in her closet.

She had once also accidentally ordered far too many pairs of slippers, when she hit the ten pairs button instead of purchasing one like she had intended. Her list of online shopping mistakes was long and vast, and she shared some of her own stories with Lauden while he set about getting the coffee made up and put into the pot. The older ceramic percolator was a throwback to a time when…well, she didn't know when.

It was always good to make yourself into an approachable person for interviews. People got pissy when it seemed like some untouchable, unfathomable force was interviewing them. They liked to know that the interviewer was on the same level as them, had hobbies and a decent enough personality. It made talking easier, conversational, and dirty details seemed more likely to be spilled.

Pilar was forced to endure the wait of the coffee being brewed, then the frantic sniffing of hound dogs when they were let in from out back.

"They don't bite," assured Lauden. "Sierra. Shiloh. And that one's Blackbird. He's an old fellow now, don't do much outside short of sit around and sleep."

The dog in question made himself at home right in front of Pilar's feet. He was big and bulky, but the skin of his face sagged and there were white hairs all about his brows and the sides of his muzzle, signaling his old age. The dog heaved out a sigh and laid his bulk against her feet. Pilar had never been very partial to dogs, but she found herself ridiculously fond of the one weighing her down.

It was probably the fact that he was old, she thought, and seemingly content in the world. He seemed the direct opposite of his owner; Pilar could tell they were nothing alike. Lauden Crenshaw had the air of a man who hadn't made too many mistakes in his life, and he didn't have any intention of making amends for those he had. Although he was clearly getting on in years, all conversation with him so far made it appear he was fine being a mostly solitary sort, and that he firmly believed it was the rest of the world that owed him, and not the other way around.

She worked her way through basic questions first.

"So, tell me about your first book." She knew the series had been met with a certain consternation from the critics, but fans loved it.

"I was in the military and used that experience to write the spy series."

"I see. I understand that some in the community thought you gave out some military secrets in the books."

"Assholes. They don't know what the fuck they're talking about. Jerkoffs."

She quickly discerned that asking about the book that gave him his original rise to fame, the sequels that came afterward, and the questionable second series that almost ended his writing career tweaked a nerve.

Each answer after that had only reinforced Pilar's original assessment of the man. He didn't talk fondly about any friends, and even references to his wife seemed cagey at best, like he wasn't respecting her as someone who had died, and didn't actually have many fond stories of her to share.

The man had a barbed tongue that would have made the crown of thorns Jesus wore look easier to twist around, thought Pilar. She was sure she could take his anger and petty righteousness and use it to bring about all sorts of juicy tidbits about Mel. All Pilar had to do now was wait for her chance.

Lauden explained, "I just went too dark with it.

Things were going rough for me with my family and the farm, and I let that bleed through too much into my writing. It wasn't my best coping mechanism, but I suppose it could have been worse. I didn't turn to drinking, at least."

"That puts you up higher than a few others I've spoken to," Pilar said.

"Oh, you know. Had a bug go through the flock of hens. Took out all of them but an old biddy that didn't lay anymore. Didn't have eggs or meat helping bring in that extra income, so our pocketbooks got a little tighter. My wife had just gotten sick—the first time around. The first time was the best and the worst, you know. She beat it, but it was hard on her. No one knew what to expect, and that made tensions thicker."

Pilar didn't know where that tidbit of information came from, but she nodded and played along. She'd done her research and knew that Mary Crenshaw had beaten cancer twice, then succumbed to it the third go-round. It was a remarkably tragic affair. An uncle of Pilar's had died from lung cancer about ten years back. She hadn't been close to him, but it had still been hard news to swallow. She meant it when she said, "I imagine that must have been hard on you."

"It was hard on all of us," Lauden agreed. He stood up, taking his empty mug with him. "Another?"

"No, thank you." Pilar liked her coffee much stronger than Lauden had brewed it. She stood up anyway, asking, "What about a tour of the farm?"

She needed to find an opening to bring up Mel. The tail end of a conversation about Lauden's dead wife was most certainly not the time for it, so she would have to do better about steering the discussion.

Lauden was amicable enough about it. He led Pilar throughout the house, steering her upstairs, pointing out where he used to have his office, explaining that after the roof started to leak he'd packed up his writing supplies and just hadn't gotten them back out.

"Seemed like too much work for something I'd already been successful at," Lauden admitted. "And I think about it some days now, but I'm getting on in years. The work around here takes me longer each day, and I just don't think I've got the time to finish anything if I started it."

"Have you ever thought about moving to the city?"

"Pfht." He snorted. "As if I would give up all of this for a claustrophobic nightmare. No offense, ma'am, but I've lived out here my whole life. My grandfather lived in this house too. It's a family home. I won't be selling it or letting the state have it until the day I'm dead and in the ground. I'll stick to trying my best to handle the farm and just leave writing to the younger crowd. Tastes have changed over the years anyhow. I doubt I could pick up any new readers even if I tried."

Odd. She'd expected a man more devoted to the memory of his dead wife. Also interesting was that he didn't seem too attached to his work, though to be as prolific and successful as he had been surely indicated a fiery passion for writing. If he had that burning impulse to write, as other authors had described to her, why wouldn't he at least try to find a new audience, or appease his existing fans? She could chalk it up to depression after Mary died—the timing of his last book coincided with her passing—but again, he talked about her as if she hadn't been more meaningful to him than those chickens he had lost. Pilar tucked that tidbit away for later. It also sounded as though Lauden had no intention of letting his daughter come back to the farm or take the house when he passed away. That had the makings of a hint about a falling out between the two of them.

Lauden seemed to enjoy showing off his home despite the fact that it was a little ragged on the edges and rough in appearance. He had chickens everywhere: on the curtains and bedspreads, on the shower cover, and sitting in every spare corner and on every shelf that they passed by. The house wasn't falling down around his ears—there weren't any visual holes and nothing smelled of rot or musty, but there were spiderwebs everywhere, and some rooms had such a thick coating of dust on them that Pilar again reckoned it must have been a good year or two since they'd last been used.

The lack of photos just made Pilar more invested in the relationship between father and daughter. Mel had been back in town for a few weeks, but it was fairly clear that she had not come back to help her aging father. That took away the more positive spin that Pilar could have put on the profile. She wasn't sure where the rest of this interview would take her.

Pilar started trying to figure out the ways she could probe for more information on Mel and her relationship with her father. There was a chance that Mel had come back to make amends with the man, but there was also a chance that she had come back despite not wanting to bridge that gap. She needed to do more digging and cheerfully suggested that she be shown the outside of the house as well.

There wasn't a lot to be gleaned from a tour of

the property. According to Lauden, he had downsized in recent years. He explained that the ten acres out back had been overgrown after the last cattle sale, since he couldn't keep up with the physical aspect of raising them and didn't want to hire any of the local boys to do it for him. Something about not trusting anyone with his property.

Supposedly, he used to own the whole five hundred acres around the house. As time had passed on, he'd sold it off in parcels, sometimes making deals with the owners to split profits of steer or hay and cut down on the initial trade cost. The farm seemed to be one of his primary interests, and Pilar kept trying to pick through his words and come up with something that was a little more interesting to listen to.

Instead, she found herself with an awful lot of knowledge about steers and property pricing, but still no stories about Mel and her siblings. That was an interesting revelation. However, Pilar found it very odd. Lauden was not the touchy type. He was obviously not any sort of soft heart. But he seemed to at least acknowledge his wife in passing during his stories of younger years, and had kept her chicken collection and continued the theme.

As for Mel, there was a strong possibility that he knew exactly why she had come back to town, and maybe he disapproved of it. That would be a great hook for the story, and might even be strong enough to take up the center mass of the article.

All Pilar had to do was suffer through the rest of the tour first.

It wasn't really a good day to be out and about. The storm clouds she'd seen earlier had become even more ominous in size and color. In Pilar's opinion, the weather was absolutely trash. The wind had not died down and whipped-up dust devils mixed with the errant hay and feathers from the chickens still pecking the ground. Despite the fact that the sun wasn't currently covered by a cloud, it was still chilly enough out for Pilar to be uncomfortable under her jacket.

After the tour of the fields and his stories, Lauden led her to a section of the property that was a little closer to the house. The ground was uneven, and the only path was a dirt one, clearly formed from walking in the same spot for countless years. Her high heels weren't a good choice for the environment, sinking in with each step. She was forced to walk several paces behind Lauden as she slowed down and watched her steps carefully in an attempt to not break her ankles or the heels off her shoes.

It was actually a relief when they made it off the path and onto solid, overgrown ground again.

The chicken coop that had once no doubt been a point of pride on the farm was run down and ragged looking, with a scant ten hens and a single rooster running about. Pilar admitted, "I've never seen chickens in person before."

That earned a guffaw from Lauden. He shook his head, clucking his tongue. "There's just something about city folk I don't get. Chickens are a dime a dozen out here. Why, you'll see them running about loose in town half the time. Strikes me as funny that you've never even seen one of them before."

Lauden reached down and picked up one, hugged it close to his body, and petted the animal. Thankfully, he didn't insist that she try to touch them. Pilar didn't like the look in their eyes. They were a little too sharp and cunning for her. They looked like little raptors, just waiting for someone's guard to be dropped.

Maybe that was a silly thought. Pilar wasn't afraid of the chickens, she just wasn't fond of animals in general. Pilar hadn't been around them much as a child, and the hesitancy that created had just never left. She was quite happy with her fish and the lone aquatic snail she kept in the tank with them. Plus, they were much cleaner than almost any other animal.

Pilar swiped at her clothes, a fine layer of dust on them just from the little bit of walking around. It was easy to see why Lauden didn't seem to mind that his pants had stains on them; new clothes and farms were clearly not a match made in heaven. Looking down at her shoes, she realized they would have to be thrown out when Pilar finally got back home.

"I'll take you around to the garden."

Great, Pilar thought.

This was clearly Lauden's major source of interest these days. The winter squash and pumpkins were growing in abundance. There were purple eggplants glinting in their thick green foliage. It was strange, seeing the vegetables out in the field like this instead of already cleaned and prettied up on a grocery store shelf.

Her mom had taken up gardening and Pilar remembered what she'd told her: "There's nothing more satisfying than growing something you can eat later. I've got a big ol' garden, but I bet you could do something even out where you live. Herbs take little more than a pot on the windowsill. It makes a difference in taste, growing it yourself."

Pilar didn't think that would be true, if only

because, well, a vegetable was a vegetable. Still, there was no denying that these plants looked larger than the ones at the grocery store. They had no blemishes, and there was something just inherently peaceful about looking at them nestled among the dirt and greenery.

He insisted on picking a few of the cucumbers and a squash for Pilar to take back, tossing them in a big plastic bag that was stuck on a wooden post. She didn't want to be disrespectful, so she took the vegetables as they walked together back around to the covered front porch.

There was a brief discussion about the exotic car that seemed to be his pride and joy—commenting on the red paint job was one last swing on Pilar's end to endear the man to her. She listened to him ramble about the vehicle for nearly ten minutes before they made it onto the porch itself. They sat across from each other in two white wooden rocking chairs and looked out over the property.

It was coming on afternoon, and she was ready to turn the conversation to the actual point of the interview. This was going to be her long shot and her wide swing. It was time to see if Pilar's patient endurance of his rambling and his tours would finally pay off.

Granted, she wasn't expecting miracles from the man. There was no doubt he wouldn't have anything nice to say about Mel. There was a chance that he wouldn't know why she had moved back here. But Pilar was certain that she would be able to get *something* usable out of the conversation.

She was good like that. Able to make a mountain out of a molehill and have it sit right on the pages.

Smooth as silk, Pilar asked, "All right, Lauden. We've talked about the books, and your wife, and your influences, but there's something else I would love to ask you about. You have a daughter that is successful in her own right."

Lauden grunted but kept his gaze looking out on the vast expanse of land.

That was a less than stellar reaction. Pilar continued all the same. "What did you think about her move to the city?"

"I think she left behind a lot of things. Things she's not going to be able to get back," Lauden said.

"It sounds like there's some resentment there. Does that have something to do with her latest difficulties?"

Lauden grunted again. Then he admitted, "I don't keep up with that too much. I always let my agent deal with the publishing houses and the press and all that nonsense. Her big-city drama and me, we don't get along."

"I don't mean difficulties in the publishing world," Pilar said. "I'm more interested in how her breakup with Jill Steele might have affected her life, or your thoughts on her."

Lauden's chair stopped rocking. His brows furrowed. "Who?"

"Her most recent girlfriend."

His mouth tugged down into a harsh-looking frown. "Girlfriend…"

That made Pilar falter. She had the sudden realization that Lauden had known nothing about the situation with Jill or about his daughter's specific romantic interests. That might have been the biggest slipup she'd made in a while.

Pilar scrambled to cover it, asking, "I suppose that means she didn't come back home to make amends with a high school sweetheart?"

Lauden's only reaction was the bobble of his Adam's apple. He sat stone-still, then shook his head and muttered something under his breath, then stood up.

"You didn't know your daughter was a lesbian?"

He looked at Pilar. His gaze razored right through her.

"That girl was never really right."

"What do you mean?"

"Nothing." He pulled at a rubber band around the arm of the rocker and let it snap a couple of times before he spoke again. "She ain't no lesbian. We might not be close since her mom died, but she's no lesbian. Her publicist tell you that?"

Pilar kept quiet, waiting for him to fill the silence.

"It's all garbage to sell books. I see all those people on facespace coming out, hoping to get more likes and keep their profiles jumping off the page. Everyone's gotta be bi, or saying they're a little gay, to attract more readers. But I'll tell you, it's a big mistake." He wagged his finger at Pilar and then snapped the rubber band again. "I should know. People live on that garbage, they eat it for breakfast, lunch, and dinner. Hell, they even have it for dessert. And it's all hogwash anyway, a damn waste of time. My daughter ain't no homo."

Wow, bigoted much? She wished she could just leave the asshole alone in his miserable existence. "So, Mel hasn't reached out to you now that she's back in town?"

"Nope."

"I see." Pilar had noticed his look had softened. "You didn't know, did you?"

"I thank you kindly for your time, but I think that's about all I can give you."

"But—"

"I've still got work to do around the farm, see," Lauden said in a steely sort of tone. "But I sure do appreciate your interest in my work."

And just like that, the interview was over. Had it been the mention of Mel that soured it? The fact that she and Jill had broken up? Or was a deeper secret revealed—had her father truly not realized that she was interested in women?

It was an abrupt end to what had been an actually fairly informative interview. She suddenly wished she was actually here to do the article on him. Reclusive writer abandons writing but still lives his glory years through memories. After a moment struggling to compose herself, Pilar nodded, stood up, and held out a hand. "It was a pleasure to talk with you."

He shook it, and then said, "Hope you have a pleasant drive back home."

Clearly, he meant back to the city, which also meant that Lauden didn't realize the interview truly hadn't been about him. That was a good thing. Pilar had no intention of going back home now, not when she was on the cusp of a breakthrough, but she didn't have any reason to tell Lauden that. Instead, she thanked him for his time, handed him her business card, and headed out toward the rental car.

Her heels were caked in red dirt by the time she made it there, her bag of vegetables in tow. She sat them down on the passenger seat, shaking her head as she backed down the long winding driveway and headed toward the lone road that led back into town. Pilar looked in her rearview mirror and watched until the frail man's image was just a small dot. She would swing by the diner that she'd seen yesterday to get something to eat, compile her notes, and make a game plan for next steps.

It seemed like this story might be bigger than she thought. Pilar wasn't positive about the exact specifics of what she was about to break open, but she had a feeling that it was going to absolutely save her career. Lauden had given her far more information than he had intended, she was certain. She wondered what other secrets Lauden Crenshaw held. No pictures of his other children, not even a mention.

Yep, he was hiding something.

And if Pilar felt a little bad for inadvertently outing Mel to her father, well, that was just something that she wasn't going to think on for the moment. News would have made it to him eventually...That was how small towns worked, right? Gossip traveled fast through small communities, especially things like that.

Riiight.

Pilar just...wasn't going to think about that one very much.

Suddenly, she felt a little sick. She told herself that it was just because she'd had so much processed food in the last twenty-four hours. It had nothing to do with spilling Mel's secrets. In an effort to distract herself, Pilar changed direction and went to the grocers.

Pulling into the parking lot, she told herself she wasn't expecting a miracle out of the store and, as expected, none was forthcoming. She did remember to grab a new phone charger, as her old one had crapped out, and she cringed when she saw it cost twice as much as it would have at home. The prices were also high for all the local produce that was grown in the area and the shelves teemed with staple food items. Didn't country folk have allergies? Was no one out here gluten intolerant? She looked down the long bread aisle stuffed to the brims with bread, pastries, and junk food.

It wasn't that big of a deal, really, but Pilar was in a bad mood and she was looking for any way to get the irritation out. Food was always a comfort for her after a tough day. This seemed like a good enough excuse to binge on crap, even if she was unjustifiably mean to the cashier over it. She wasn't in a better mood by the time she finished, but at least she wasn't feeling sick anymore.

Pilar just needed to focus on the task at hand. Otherwise, she might recognize that tinge of guilt eating at the pit of her stomach.

Chapter Six

By the time that the phone rang for the fourth time that day, Mel was more than frazzled. She didn't even check the caller ID before picking it up and answering with a harsh, "What?"

Her father's voice filtered over the line. "Is that what you learned in the city? How to lose all your manners and turn into a piece of work on the phone?"

"Dad?"

"I need you to get your rear in gear and get out here," Lauden demanded.

Worry gnawed at Mel as she asked, "Is everything okay?"

"Just get out here," Lauden repeated. "Today, if you've got half a mind to be useful."

Mel was frozen in her confliction. She hadn't even bothered to let her father know she was in town, so the call surprised her. After her mother's death, they hadn't spoken but a few sentences after the funeral. Truth be told, she didn't get along very well with her father, despite her initial best efforts to comfort him after losing her mom. His views on life were too different, and time had only made their relationship worse, not better. Her mother had been his world, and he'd pushed his kids away, acting as if they didn't exist. His harsh words had destroyed her sisters and brother after Mary's death. He practically blamed them all for the loss of her. Cancer was an evil villain. Her father was worse, though, and he took it out on those closest to him.

Bastard.

Mel could only imagine that something must have been dreadfully wrong for him to call her up like that and demand she come over. Thoughts of the day that they received news of her mother's illness were brought to the surface of Mel's mind like a storm cloud brought in on the hard, packed dirt. Why she called and canceled the plans that she had made with the handyman was beyond her. She didn't owe the sperm donor anything. Yet she cited a family emergency, which she was certain it must be, and rescheduled for tomorrow.

"Thanks for understanding, Andy. Yeah, I know that water heater isn't going to fix itself, but something came up out at my dad's farm, so I need to go out there and help."

"I can come by and fix it if you just leave the keys on the deck somewhere."

"Seriously?"

"Sure, unless you got a Rembrandt or something you are worried about?"

She gave a nervous laugh. Mel had left anything of value at the city house, so that wasn't it. She just wasn't used to the laid-back nature of country people anymore.

"Nah, I spent my inheritance on drugs and booze."

"That a girl. Can't take it with you."

They both laughed.

"That would be great. Thanks Andy, I owe you."

"No problem. Tell your dad I have that new sprinkler system coming in next week."

"Will do, thanks again."

She grabbed her keys, pulled on her boots, and headed out to her father's ranch. A long time ago, the ranch itself had been home to Mel. She had come here seeking sanctuary in the darkness of the nearby pine trees and the openness of the cattle fields. Her youth had been spent hiding from chores inside of the chicken coop and pulling weeds in the garden.

"Assholes and elbows, girls. I want those weeds gone by the end of the day," she remembered her mom saying as they all worked in the garden.

She had loved the farm.

Her parents' house didn't feel like home anymore and definitely not like the safe haven her mother had created for her kids. With the purchase of her own ranch, she hoped she'd be able to recreate that warm, loving sanctuary her mother had created for her. A place where she felt she finally belonged.

Comfort seemed in short supply lately, especially after the mess she'd made of her life. Even writing didn't seem to give her the comfort and cover she so desperately craved.

As she drove slowly up the long winding driveway toward the old farmhouse, guilt bit at the back of Mel's mind. It was hard to ignore the fact that the farm had seen better days. The fields were overgrown; the fences lining the property and the various fields were all in dire need of repair and a good paint job. Mel jabbed at the keypad and waited for the gate to crawl open.

That was the sort of thing she would have been helping with if her father weren't such an asshole. A part of Mel wondered if maybe that was what this talk was going to be about. Maybe it wasn't about someone being sick. Maybe it was about her father getting old, about him wanting more help, about him being glad that she had moved back into town and maybe, just maybe, she held out hope he wanted help to repair not just the farm, but their relationship too.

It was a long shot, but Mel clung to that as she parked the truck and got out.

Blackbird rose from his place in a sunspot on the porch and hurried over to see her, pressing his wet nose into the palm of Mel's hand and wagging his tail something fierce.

"It's good to see you too, old man," Mel said happily. She took a few minutes to stand there and pet the elderly hound, then started up the steps and into the house. The front door opened before she had even finished crossing the porch.

Sounding sour, Lauden gruffed, "It's about time. I thought you might not actually show up."

"You told me to come out. How did you know I was back?" Mel followed her father into the house. It still had that woodsy smell to it she'd always loved and never been able to replicate no matter what candles, incense, or oils she mixed and lit up.

"I tell you a lot of things. That's never stopped you before. I figure you just ignore it, just out of pure spite."

"I'm not the one who says shit out of spite, Lauden," Mel said defensively. "Just because I decided to go after a career—" She paused, pinched the bridge of her nose, and drew in a deep breath. "No. I'm not doing that. I didn't come out here to fight with you over the past. Tell me that's not all you wanted me to drive out here for?"

"Nope. I'm not rightly interested in the past

at the moment. I'm more interested in the present. You didn't see fit to tell me anything, so I didn't ask anything when you showed back up around here. I figured maybe you had just finally gotten some common sense and realized here is where you belonged."

That stung a bit, if only because Mel wasn't entirely sure where she belonged at the moment. Both the city and the country seemed to offer too many and too few options. The lines between everything had gotten blurred recently, and she wasn't too happy about that. She certainly wasn't going to spill all those insecurities to her father.

Mel had never been particularly close to Lauden. He wasn't the sort of warm and fuzzy father figure that someone was able to talk feelings with. That had been her mother's job. He'd always been gruff and distant, even when Mel had been a little girl. He hadn't softened over the years.

This sounded like the start of a family squabble and Mel felt blindsided at the sudden request from her father. She couldn't imagine what anyone might have told him in town to cause this stir, assuming that was why Mel was summoned. She'd been careful about who she spoke to and what she'd told them about her reasons for being back.

Grasping at straws, she asked, "Is this about me buying that old house? I'm more than capable of fixing it up, you know. I've already made a lot of progress on it. You're welcome to come by sometime if you don't believe me. Get a gander at it, see if my work is up to your approval."

"I'm not interested in your house!" Lauden spun around to face her, voice pitched low and angry. His cheeks were faintly red when he said, "I'll be honest with you, Mel, which is more than I can say you've been with me."

"What are you talking about? I haven't lied to you about anything. In fact, I haven't spoken to you in years, so what's this about?"

"Let's just cut to the chase, then. What's this I hear about you being a woman chaser? A lesbian."

The accusation seemed to come from nowhere and caught Mel completely off guard. Woman chaser? As in, she was interested in a woman? That she was gay?

It felt like a pit had just opened up underneath her feet and she was hanging perilously above, ready to be dropped in. In all honesty, Mel hadn't really planned on telling her father anything about her romantic life. She certainly wasn't going to do it now, not when Mel herself wasn't certain what the next step was supposed to be, and Jill and Carrie and now even Pilar were looming behind her like rabid dogs just waiting to be let off the leash long enough to pounce.

But here they were. Had that really just come out of his mouth?

Floundering, Mel denied it out of instinct. "My personal life is none of your business."

"So you haven't been going around having relations with women?"

"Relations? Dad, you know what year it is, right? No one uses that term anymore."

"That's not an answer, now is it?"

"Why are you even asking this?" Mel was desperately hoping that she could change the subject without it being too obvious, and that he would let the whole thing go. Maybe forever, but at least until later.

Lauden Crenshaw, however, was not a man who could easily be distracted. "Tell me you weren't caught sleeping around with a woman named Jill Steele."

It wasn't a question. It was a demand.

Mel had never felt so small in her life. Whatever family emergencies she had been bracing herself to deal with, something like her love life being brought to light had never crossed her mind. And now it appeared she had two choices.

She could, of course, continue to lie to her father. She could say exactly what Lauden wanted to hear: that it was a tabloid lie made up to sully her name, that it was someone trying to come after her money, that she was completely straight. Mel had friends. She could easily play the card about having a boyfriend who lived in the city and hated to travel, thus he could never come out and meet her father. Truth was, she didn't want anyone meeting her father anyway.

She could also, of course, tell the truth. She could admit that she loved women, and that she had known for a long time. Mel could say that her mother already knew—lie or truth, it wouldn't matter. There was no one around anymore to contradict it. She could tell him exactly how bad the relationship with Jill had gone, and how she was struggling to figure out her next steps.

A part of Mel knew that if she told Lauden, he was going to hate her. He hated "fags," as he called people like her. He'd made that known more than once when she was growing up. That's what pushed her to move away when she was younger. She'd rather slit her wrist than endure his disapproval.

Lauden Crenshaw was an opinionated, unforgiving man. He was old-fashioned in the worst sort of way. He would hear the story, and there was no doubt in her mind that he was going to be angry. But the thought of living a lie for the rest of her life seemed utterly miserable, especially when she herself was struggling with if and how to mend their relationship. How could she think she could even start to do that if she kept lying to him?

She said, calmly as she could, "Yes, Dad. I love women. I'm a lesbian. I've known for a long time and…I don't know how you found out, but—"

She shut her mouth as she was interrupted by the man, who was never at a loss for words. They were his stock-in-trade, and he bandied them about like a needle-sharp sword meant to wound when they hit their target. She never knew what her mother saw in the now frail old bastard, and she didn't have time to guess again. He grabbed the worn trucker hat from his head and slammed it down in the center of the table. "She was right."

She?

A sudden bolt of realization shot through Mel. This was that reporter's fault. She had gone poking her nose into places it didn't belong, and this was the result.

Mel barely had time to register her anger at Pilar Stein before she was quickly crushed beneath the steely anger of her father's gaze. "You tell me right now what the hell you were thinking."

Mel, surprised, sputtered, "What?"

"You heard me. Tell me what's going on in that brain of yours. What made you think this was a good idea." It wasn't a question. It was a cold, hard demand. The anger on her father's face was impossible to ignore. It flashed in his eyes, hot like fire, and made his cheeks red and the vein in the side of his thick neck bulge out as it always did when he was angry.

In that moment—hell, at any time—Mel's father could make her feel smaller than anything else had ever made her feel. She felt like she should just lie down and never get back up. For a brief moment, Mel contemplated just turning and leaving right then, before it could turn into a huge fight. That moment passed in a blink, however.

Mel decided it was time she stood up for herself. He'd made his choices in his life when it came to his relationship with her and her siblings, so she was going to lay on the honesty about her own life choices whether he liked it or not. Now she had to stand her ground and…what, defend herself? She would hope that she could convince Lauden to not be a prejudiced old man who was still living in the past.

Ultimately, she guessed she would have to settle for a bigoted father, but she wouldn't let his judgment rest on her.

Mel took a deep breath. Then she told him, "I haven't been thinking about anything, Dad. I've known for a long time. I told Mom about it, and she was okay with it."

"Bullshit."

"Seriously, you're calling *me* a liar? That's rich, especially when it comes to Mom. The only reason I never told you was because of…this right here. I knew you would never understand. I knew you would just do what you always do—be a judgmental prick."

"What I always do? Judgmental prick? How dare you? I'm your father and I deserve the respect due of a father."

Mel laughed. "You can't be serious. You have

some nerve calling me and demanding I attend an audience with the great Lauden Crenshaw. See, I knew you would get pissed, when there's absolutely no reason for you to be pissed. This is my life, not yours."

Lauden snorted and shook his head. He looked like he was tempted to slam something else down onto the table, but didn't have anything within easy reach so he slammed his fists on the counter, making her lean back. "No reason? Of course there's a reason. This is why you came back, isn't it? Because you know that it's gone and ruined your career. Ruined your life, because you couldn't think like a normal person."

"I am a normal person." Mel's face felt heated. Tears were pricking at her eyes, but she refused to cry in front of her father. Not this time. Not today. She would not give him that satisfaction.

Lauden, spitting mad, said, "I had to find out from that journalist and not from my own daughter. You need to just tell that woman doing the article that it was a mistake. A one-off accident, and it didn't mean nothing. That's the only way you're ever going to get back on your feet."

Her suspicions were confirmed. This was Pilar Stein's fault. The sheer anger that Mel felt toward that woman was second only to the grief caused by this conversation.

"What did you say to her, Lauden? And by the way, it wasn't a mistake. I mean, that relationship may not have ended well, but it wasn't a mistake. We all have breakups, and this one was messy. But the fact that I like women, that's not a mistake, and it's not something I'm going to apologize for."

"Then get out. No daughter of mine is gay." Lauden's voice was like ice.

Mel froze. Her breath caught in her throat. Her voice sounded eerily calm when she asked, "What?"

"You heard me," Lauden said. "If you can't admit to your mistakes—"

"It wasn't a mistake," insisted Mel. She stood and owned her space in this house and her world. Her father's opinion of her would not change who she was, and she wasn't about to kowtow to his ideas of what a woman was or should be. "It's my life, and I'll live it how I want. I will not pretend to be someone I'm not just because it makes you uncomfortable. Which is beyond ironic, I might add. I will not die with regrets like Mom did."

The last part slipped out before she could take it back. She hadn't meant to say it, but it was real and honest. Clearly, he didn't know her mom like Mel did, but she'd spent too long denying herself just for her father to force her back into the closet.

Still, she wasn't prepared for the way it felt to hear him say, "Then get the hell out of this house, and don't bother coming back. I don't care what your mamma said. You're not welcome in my home."

The words cut deep. They cut deeper than Mel thought they would. She gave him a firm nod and said, "I suppose that's your choice. You know, Lauden, ask yourself why you're alone and none of your kids give you the time of day. But at your age, I guess it doesn't matter. You're going to die an old, lonely man." And then she turned and marched out of the living room, looking around for what she knew would be the last time. As she walked out onto the porch, a flood of childhood memories assaulted her. Her mother and her sitting on the swing as the day closed, talking about life, dreams, and the future.

Blackbird was still sitting by the truck. He perked up when Mel came toward him, but she didn't stop to pet the dog. It was something that she might regret later, not giving the old hound a proper goodbye. In that moment, though, Mel's only focus was on getting off the property before she gave in and cried. She had to put distance between herself and her father.

So she walked right past Blackbird and got into her truck. She turned the key and backed down the driveway, then pulled out onto the main road. The radio was still turned on, blaring music from the drive out there. She had never felt so sick, numb, and distant. She had let her father get to her, and it sickened her more. It was like someone else was controlling her body and moving her on autopilot. She didn't even realize where she was going until she was pulling into the driveway of her own house. The sun was setting and the impending storm outside was just as chilling as it was on the inside. The clouds gathering were an exact reflection on the inner storm building in Mel.

The pain in her chest made her lungs ache. Or maybe that was the fact that she was crying? Mel didn't know when she had started crying, only that the tears were leaving hot tracks down her cheeks as she shut off the engine and got out of the truck.

She stood there for a moment, hoping that the cold of the oncoming winter night might help bring her senses back to her. The sky wasn't dark just because of the early setting sun. That winter storm they had all been expecting was going to break soon, and the air was heavy with clouds.

A part of Mel was very focused on the fact that she wasn't ready for the storm. There were still leaking parts on the roof. The hot water tank still didn't work.

Mel hadn't gone to town to stock up on gallons of water or nonperishables. She still had a lot to do. Mel should have stayed home and supervised the work Andy was doing on the water heater. Looking around, she realized she should never have bought this house.

It was easier to think about the storm and her lack of supplies than anything else. The storm was a physical problem, with straightforward solutions. Go to the store, try to speed up the process of getting the handyman out to help finish with the repairs. Her need for a sanctuary was replaced with anger and frustration. What was she thinking coming back home?

She might not have done this for a long damn time, but the routine was still there. Put the blankets somewhere easy to access. Make sure there was food that could be fixed without power and get bottled water on the shelf. Keep all your warm clothes as clean as possible. That made sense. Not only did it make sense, but it was a good distraction.

Problem. Solution. It was how her mind worked. Now she had an additional problem: Pilar Stein.

The rest of Mel was well aware of the fact that standing outside in the cold wasn't getting anything done. It sure wasn't making her feel better. If anything, the cold and the shivers now racking her body made Mel feel worse. It was like she was held together with duct tape and glue, string and thumbtacks the only things keeping her all in one place.

There seemed to be no solution to this particular issue with her dad. The fact that he had been so willing to turn her away and tell her to never come back was the closing chapter in her relationship with her father. Had he just been waiting for a chance to say that? Had this been an opening that he'd been looking for to cut her out of his life? Thinking about it that way was somehow worse. Mel knew that she and her father didn't have the best relationship, but the fact that it was just gone…it set off an empty, aching longing in her chest. The loss of her mother had been catastrophic. Would she have given anything to go back and redo that conversation? Why hadn't she just lied to him? That would have saved them both a lot of grief. They could have gone on pretending to love each other, gone on pretending that they were a good, healthy, stable family. Not without her mom. She was the peacekeeper in the family, the salve that kept families together. At least, families like hers.

Now, that was gone. There was no way that this wouldn't spread through town like fire in a hayloft. Within a matter of days, everyone would know— not just that she was gay, but that she was an awful daughter and her father wanted nothing to do with her.

She had officially been disowned. The word seemed to echo in her mind. It was a realization that she hadn't fully made yet, but a true one all the same.

Mel didn't have any family left in town. Her father—no, Lauden, as he wanted it—made it clear enough.

Mel gave her head a hard shake and then hurried into the house. Closing the door behind her cut off the wind, but she couldn't shake the cold that lanced through her body. Mel hurried to turn on the small space heater in the living room, opting to sit on the floor in front of it instead of on the couch.

She lost track of how long she sat there basking in the warmth of the heater, crying, and trying to sort out the mess in her brain. It shouldn't have hurt so badly to have her father turn his back on her like that. They had never been close, but the finality of it all stung horribly.

Maybe it was because her mother had spent so many years in that house and now Mel would never be able to go in there again.

How dare he? After everything her mother had done, had sacrificed, how *dare* he?

Maybe it was the fact that it hadn't been on her own terms.

That last thought was finally enough to make the grief dissolve, replacing it with the absolute rage that Pilar Stein would dare do something like this. Mel wasn't going to take it lying down.

Now that she was warmer and thinking more clearly, Mel knew that there was only one thing left she could do. She was going to confront Pilar Stein and get to the bottom of this. She needed to show the reporter the proverbial door—and make sure that she left town with no desire to pursue any story about the Crenshaw family.

More determined than ever, Mel abandoned her post by the heater in favor of going upstairs. It was even colder in the second-floor hallway. She could see her breath.

"Where did I put that number?" she muttered to herself.

The room was a disaster. Between repairs, work, and trying to unpack, it seemed like there wasn't an organized place in the whole damn house outside of her office. The mattress, which was piled full of both clothes and papers, stood as a monument to her madness at the moment. She finally found the business card with Pilar's number on it on her dresser, half shoved underneath a how-to manual for water heaters. Mel grabbed the card and a blanket from the bed, then scurried back downstairs to the still chilly but much, much warmer living room.

Despite the late hour, Mel called the number on the back of the card. Predictably, it went to voicemail.

Sounding far calmer than she felt, Mel said, "All right, Ms. Stein. That's it. I'll meet you tomorrow morning at the local diner, alone." She didn't know why she added to that last part—she knew the woman was alone. With a little more authority in her voice, she added, "Be there if you want to talk."

Chapter Seven

In the hotel room, with the new charger connected and her cell phone still powered off while it struggled to get enough energy into it, Pilar got started sorting out all the details of her article in her head while she prepared food.

The TV dinner she had bought wasn't great, but it was slightly better than vending machine fare. She nibbled at the veggie chips she'd found in the small health food section of the grocery story as she watched her TV dinner spin on the microwave carousel. They cost twice as much as they should have, but she hadn't been able to resist. Pilar needed to feel like she was eating something at least *vaguely* healthy. Her mind wandered to Mel Crenshaw as she waited. She was starting to understand why Mel had tried to keep her personal life personal. Growing up in a bigoted house couldn't have been easy for the woman. Her father definitely didn't seem like the accepting type if you strayed outside his value system. The microwave dinged.

With her dinner done, Pilar was content to turn her attention toward the article and the work in front of her. Well, content wasn't the right word for it. More like there was only so much Pilar could find to satisfy her need for productivity in the small, claustrophobic room.

She flipped through the photos of Mel Crenshaw

on her computer. Some had been provided by her editor, and some of them had been taken recently by the PI she had hired. They would give the story a nice visual complement. A lot of them were older, most of her high-profile events surrounding book releases, author appearances, and awards ceremonies. She looked happy, smiling as she interacted with her adoring fans. Typical book signings and meet-and-greets that authors had when a new novel dropped.

If Pilar were being honest with herself, she had to admit Melanie Crenshaw was drop-dead gorgeous. Pillar had a type, and Melanie checked all the boxes: attractive, creative, smart, with a rockin' body and a smile that brightened a room.

Wonder what she's like in bed. Damn, did she really just let that thought out into the universe? She smiled. She was only sorry that the article meant that she would never find out. Then again, maybe if she… Naw, that was a dead end, for sure.

Pilar started sorting the pictures in order, putting the most recent ones at the front of the line and going backward in time as she went on. Most of the pictures that featured Mel as a youth were either from local events that had made it into the newspaper, or happened to be pictures of Mel with her mother that had been dug up during previous attempts to find something in Mel's life worth making into a cover piece.

The dead mother card had never sat right with Pilar. It wasn't stunning, either. Best that she could tell, every source claimed that Mel and her mother had been close when the woman passed away. Whatever issues they might have had were well since worked out. What was missing in the group were photos of

Mel with her father. The famous elder didn't seem to play a role in any events, and she suspected jealousy might have been at the root of the missing man.

It was odd, though, she thought as she browsed through the collection.

But, Mel's father had given her plenty to run with during her visit. Magdalena was a sucker for hard-hitting profiles that gave the reader new information about the subject. Mel Crenshaw being estranged from her father because of her sexuality would be a scoop, no doubt.

But now there was something else that sat wrong with her. The lesbian angle was hot, and it would certainly blow the lid off the story. In fact, Pilar was certain that she could even name her own price for it, especially if she wrote it as an exposé and shopped it to the tabloids. She sure could use the exposure, even if that type of work wouldn't land her the respect she'd been working toward re-capturing.

The problem was, it felt…wrong.

That ugly little thing called a conscience bubbled up when Pilar thought about using this angle as the cornerstone of her article, even in a cover story for the *Literary Times.* Something like this would dominate the market and get her name on the radar of pretty much everything, but the LGBT groups would come gunning for her if she used it.

Still, it was a part of Mel Crenshaw's life that she and her publishers had kept from the world. Any hint of it was immediately squashed on the blogs, news articles, and interviews she'd done over the years. Brand management was a PR nightmare for those who lived in the limelight of the literary world. The problem was that it also felt like one of the most compromising breaches of ethics out there. Sure, there weren't any set rules about this sort of thing. Honestly, it didn't even have any unspoken rules attached to it, but it still felt like the wrong thing to do. The LGBT community would latch on to Mel Crenshaw as the poster child for American hypocrisy when it came to outing someone.

Pilar already felt like shit for accidentally dropping that bombshell on Lauden. Could she really do it again, but on a national media scale?

On some level it seemed distasteful, and if she was being honest, it was starting to leave a bad taste in her mouth.

Pilar shuffled through the pictures, renaming them and putting them in a particular order for the article, and then closed the password-protected folder she kept them in for safekeeping. She started to put up the papers and the notes, clearing off the uncomfortable motel bed so she could settle back in for another long night of unrestful sleep.

Once the bed was cleared off, she stepped into the bathroom and took a shower. The water smelled pungent, like sulfur. There wasn't enough water pressure, and the temperature controls were incredibly sensitive and hard to navigate. It was a quick shower, just like all the rest had been.

When Pilar got out, her mind was no clearer than before the shower. There still was no obvious answer to the question. She dragged out her after-shower routine and got dressed in her pajamas: a soft set of pants and an old T-shirt from her college days. Then she made a trip out to the vending machine, again. Her sweet tooth needed to be squelched.

She tried to get out a honey bun, but the whole

thing jammed up. No amount of beating against it managed to procure the treat, or her dollar fifty. It felt like some sort of bad omen. As soon as that thought crossed Pilar's mind she shook her head, scolded herself for being superstitious, then marched herself back into the room.

"This is ridiculous," she announced to herself.

The choice was obvious. Pilar would need to speak to Mel in person and offer her the opportunity to review—or even rewrite—the article. Would Mel agree? The same charm she used to get to Lauden would need to be doubled, probably tripled, if she was going to get Mel to open up. Suddenly, she felt bad for Mel. Just thinking about tricking and charming the other woman made her nauseous.

Guilt wasn't Pilar's usual style. Was just the genteel nature of the country town getting to her? Maybe she was just tired. She would have a better outlook on everything in the morning, after she got some much-needed sleep.

Decision made, Pilar climbed into bed and pulled the scratchy sheets up over her shoulders. She took a deep breath, held it to the count of ten, and let it back out on an exhale.

It would be all right. She could handle this just fine, she told herself. In the morning, she would have a better grip on things.

Pilar did not sleep easily. She tossed and turned all night. Her dreams were wild and haunted, replaying the bigoted remarks from Lauden Crenshaw. Every time she woke up she went to write them down, but they vanished into the night air. The lack of sound was getting to her. She was used to the noise of cars rushing past, nondescript conversations on the street, and the occasional barking of her neighbor's dog. It was an urban symphony she was used to that helped her sleep.

Normally, Pilar stayed in suites, or in hotels with four-star reputations, at least. Places where no matter how thick the walls, there were always going to be cars rushing past outside, lights flashing in through the curtains, painting the walls.

There were always people just outside the door, talking and laughing, moving on to places of their own. Hell, even the occasional headboard thumper wouldn't have been missed.

Instead, the television was the only light flashing, and the only sound that could occasionally be heard was the static sometimes breaking away to whatever infomercial was on at the time. It wasn't like Pilar to need some sort of night-light, but the whole situation had her rattled and a little more out of sorts than usual.

It was a long and uneasy night, that was for sure. Pilar could only hope that the next morning would offer an opportunity to talk to Mel Crenshaw and get out of town.

Chapter Eight

The confrontation with her father had thoroughly stripped away any chances that the rest of the evening might be salvageable. And, oh, Mel had tried. She had turned her attention to prepping for the oncoming storm, but no amount of thinking, sorting, or trying to distract herself could work.

Had her father given the journalist enough for her story? Had he confirmed everything Pilar Stein wanted to know about his daughter? The thoughts rambled nonstop through her head. Mel kept finding herself distracted, standing and staring at nothing, an outright wasting away of the evening. At some point, Mel decided that it just wasn't worth the effort and turned to a different means of distracting herself. Was it a better means? Was it a healthier way to do it? Probably not. But hey, sometimes you just had to be unhealthy and selfish. Today was one of those days.

By midnight, Mel was definitely drunk to distraction. It wasn't a light sort of drunk, either, like when you had a few too many beers or polished off a bottle of wine that you shouldn't have finished. It was the sort of drunk that Mel hadn't been in years, with a cheap bottle of bourbon that was empty, and the bottom of the second in sight.

Mel had brought the little space heater, the bourbon, a box of crackers, an assortment of junk food, and her blankets up into the bedroom and made a nest out of them on the bed. Unwilling to put away anything on the bed that night, she had opted to position all the surrounding pillows instead, sitting in the middle of the messy pile.

It actually wasn't as uncomfortable as it had looked. She was content to curl up in her little nest as she ate her way through the majority of the snack food that she had packed up. When she was ready to sober up, she would find that hot chocolate she'd packed down in the boxes in the kitchen.

Maybe.

Suddenly, it felt like the right time to exorcise her demons. At the start of the night, Mel had been hoping it would calm her nerves enough that she could think clearly about the matter at hand. Now, though, it felt as though the opposite had happened. Mel was even more agitated than before and trapped in an awful loop of thoughts that only heightened her anxiety and frustration with Pilar Stein.

The woman, surely, was the devil incarnate.

Except that just the thought of demons made Mel burst out into laughter. That was what her very religious father might say: how she was a parasite, scum brought to earth by the devil to test wiles and push at all societies' buttons. The fact that Mel was thinking like him, even so abstractly, made her both break into hysterics and want to be sick all at the same time.

In a stunning dichotomy, she ended up laughing until she was crying again, and then drinking even more until she had stopped crying. The morning might bring a choice Mel would come to regret, but she would deal with that later. However, at that moment, drinking seemed to be the only thing holding her together.

There weren't even any good distractions in this house. There was no television hooked up yet, and the storm had the radio coming in spotty. She'd finished watching everything she'd downloaded to her tablet. The storm wasn't doing any wonders for the internet on her phone, either. Pages would load, or at least the writing did. The pictures seemed completely lost to the void, however. As the storm clouds continued to gather outside, the service got worse and worse, until the act of waiting for a page to load was enough to make Mel want to pitch her phone across the room.

That, of course, meant that drinking really was her only option. It wasn't just a reaction to a bad situation, it was the only action available.

Two more shots of bourbon and Mel had a brilliant idea. She might not be able to think about how to properly handle the situation, but there was one person who Mel was certain could help.

Fumbling with her phone and trying twice before she succeeded, Mel called the only person around.

Emily.

Emily sounded like she'd been sleeping—like any reasonable person would at this hour—when she answered. "Mel? Is something wrong?"

"Yes," Mel slurred. "Well, no. But yes."

"Are you...drunk?"

"I'm most certainly getting there."

"What's wrong...did something happen?" Emily said, yawning into the receiver.

Mel briefly felt bad about the situation. She wasn't known for calling and waking Emily up in the middle of the night, but guilt was quickly overridden by the need to bring someone else into her panic and malaise.

Without thinking, Mel spilled the details. She told Emily everything, even things she knew Emily already knew, from how Jill was acting, to the fact that Pilar Stein had followed her down to the country. Then, with a shaking voice from the liquid courage, Mel spilled the details of the journalist outing her to Lauden and what had happened when she was summoned to her father's ranch afterward.

"She didn't." Emily gasped.

"She did."

"Mel. No."

"Yes."

"Shit, shit, shit. Okay, look, I can do damage control."

Mel paused. She actually hadn't been calling for anything more than a sympathetic ear to talk to, and maybe a shoulder to cry on. A little "it will be all right" was what she was after.

"Damage control?"

"Not tonight, obviously," Emily said. "But I can come down to the farm tomorrow and handle the pending media invasion."

Oh, if that wasn't just the sweetest thing that Mel had ever heard. She gave a very loud, very wet sniff.

Emily all but cooed, "Don't cry, Mel. It's going to be all right."

"I don't know how..." Mel started but then she stopped herself, scrubbed at her face with the back of her hand, and took another swig of bourbon. "I don't want you to come out here. Not yet, at least. I'll figure something out. I just wanted someone else to know,

I guess. I just—I'm sorry, it's late, I shouldn't have bothered you."

"You didn't bother me," Emily said firmly. "We're friends, and there's nothing you could have done or said that would make me upset about you calling me. I don't mind coming out there. You know I'm good with PR."

"I have to talk to her," Mel said. "I'm going to. Tomorrow."

"Mel…I'm not sure that's a good idea."

"I think it's the only way to get her to stop."

"Are you sure that's how you want to handle it?"

"I think so. I don't know…what the hell am I going to say?" Mel said, frustrated. "I just want—I don't know. I just know that I need to talk to her. I need to be able to look her in the eyes when I tell her off."

"If that will make you feel better, but as your friend, I don't think that's a good idea. The more you deny it, the deeper she'll dig." Emily sounded doubtful that it would help. She was probably right. Mel would likely make an even bigger mess of things when all she wanted was for the woman to leave her alone in her pain and torment. Pilar Stein was directly responsible for at least the issues with her parental unit.

Emily was easy to talk to and, honestly, it was nice to talk to someone who had a vested interest in her well-being. She secretly thought Emily might have a crush on her and, truth be told, if she were younger she just might have had one on Emily too. It would never work now, however, so she'd kept it professional with Emily. An administrative assistant was privy to some of the most intimate details of a writer's life, so arm's length was exactly right. Fuck, she'd think about it later.

"You know, I can come if you need me," Emily said again, her voice hopeful.

"I don't want you to have to come all the way out here, Em." Part of her wanted to say yes, pleased at the prospect of company, but her place was barely fit for her to live there.

"I don't mind, Mel, really."

"Let me see how things work out with Pilar Stein first. I might need bail money if it goes south."

"Mel…" Emily warned. "Oh, before I forget, I was able to talk to my reporter friend, who gave me some juicy bits about Pilar Stein."

"Really?"

The more Emily shared, the more confident she became that she'd be able to get Pilar Stein off her back.

"This is great, Em. I'm not sure if I'll use it. That would make me like her…but, hey, if she doesn't drop it all, I can't be responsible for what happens next."

"No violence. Besides, one crisis per year. I can only do so much damage control and you don't want to live in the tabloids, do you?"

"No, you're right. I've had my fill of paper drama for a while."

"By the way, Jill called, again—"

"Tell that bitch to go pound sand. She's the whole reason I'm in this mess."

"I said it a little nicer. She said she was going to call back and if you didn't call her, she was going to send out the dogs."

"Hmm."

"I'll…" Emily yawned. "Call in the morning and see how you're doing."

"Thanks, Em. I don't know what I would do without you talking me off the ledge."

"Remember that when it comes time for my Christmas bonus."

"Do I give those?"

"Hardy, har, har. I'll talk to you in the morning."

"Don't call too early. I suspect I'll have the mother of all hangovers."

"Drink lots of water, take two aspirin, and eat something before you go to bed."

"I will."

"Promise?"

"Promise."

Both said bye in unison before the line went dead.

She thought she was ready to face the silence of the house again, but Mel quickly found that was the opposite. It seemed even more quiet than before.

Mel had to do something to distract herself.

Bringing her bottle of bourbon with her, she staggered into her office. The files for her novel were sitting open on the computer, mocking her. The printed copy of what she had sat out on the desk marked up with her red notes. Now they looked like someone had bled all over them.

Mel swallowed hard, past a lump in her throat, and set to work pulling up a new, empty Word document. She would just have to figure out what to say to Pilar, it seemed.

Mel could do that. She could control the message even if she couldn't control the messenger.

Chapter Nine

The curtains, with their vast amount of moth holes did little to keep the burgeoning sunlight from waking her up. Yeah, she needed to find better arrangements or she was going to go crazy. Pilar usually got up early, but this was crazy. Pilar reached for her cell phone. She'd forgotten to turn it on before going to bed, probably why she was awake so early. It was an addiction, no doubt. There was no way she could live without it, and she knew it. It was her lifeline to everything in her world. As it powered on, the message app flashed. While she didn't recognize the number, the voice she knew.

Mel Crenshaw was demanding a meeting with her. Her agitated voice boomed in the message. However, while she should be thrilled at the invitation, Pilar was nervous. What made Mel change her mind? It didn't matter; she was going to meet Mel and get this interview over and done with so she could put this godforsaken town in her rearview mirror.

Pilar laid out her clothes, assessed them, and then pulled out another outfit. This time she picked a pair of tight jeans, a form fitting sweater, and a sleek pair of pumps. Staring at the outfit, she knew the ensemble was eye catching and flattering on her, but she was meeting a woman who was hurting, so why was she picking sexy over function? Sorting through her suitcase, it was clear her options were limited.

She'd only packed for a few days at most, so what she was left with was a sundress and dress slacks. Pulling open the curtains, her choice was made for her when she saw the pavement glistening in the gray morning sunlight. Sweater and jeans. Her favorite dress was obviously not appropriate for the dreary weather. That left a sour taste in Pilar's mouth, and her attitude was spiraling downward as well.

A sponge bath was the best she could do as she couldn't bring herself to take another foul-smelling shower. Spritzing herself with cologne, she packed up her things, deciding that one way or the other this would be the last day that she spent in town. Then she decided that she might as well go to the diner early and get something to eat that was decent. Or at least more decent than honey buns and crap coffee in the motel lobby.

Honestly, Pilar had little hope for the diner, either.

She stepped out of the motel and made her way to the car, dodging puddles and mud. She was surprised by how quickly the day was turning dark. The sky was heavy with clouds, and the air was stronger and more biting than it had been the day before. Pilar found herself regretting not bringing a heavier, thicker coat along with her. The day seemed to be off to a bad start already. She could only hope that this didn't continue all throughout the rest of the day. Pulling her phone, she tapped in her route home and set it. She didn't want to waste any time getting out of town as soon as her interview with Mel was finished.

Pilar cranked on the heater the minute she started the rental, setting it as high as she could. Then she made her way toward the diner. It was still surprising to Pilar how quiet the town seemed. While she hated stereotypes, all the things said about country life being slow were true. No one seemed to be in a hurry except her. Yep, country life was just that: slow. She was still surprised there wasn't something happening on every street corner. No sidewalk vendors, no coffee carts, not even the occasional dog walker.

Pilar was a city girl, born and bred. This wasn't the first time that she had traveled in search of the good juicy parts of a story, but it was certainly the first time that she had gone quite so far out of the way of modern conveniences.

It felt a bit like a mistake, really. The country might have been too quiet to give up any of its secrets, but that wouldn't put her off her mission. Pilar wouldn't drop the story. She just couldn't. Her entire career seemed to rely on whether this one article was actually going to get off the ground and hit big. But so far, the country had only offered her a short glimpse of simple people with down-home values, like the flags hanging off almost all the business, dogs behind fences, and kids walking to the school bus waiting for them.

Pilar strummed her fingers against the steering wheel. She still hadn't decided what she was going to do with the lesbian angle on the story. The reporter in her was a vicious lion, grabbing the juicy details and holding on tight. But the rest of her just felt bad for even considering using that as the centerpiece for the profile. She really didn't want to be known as the woman who outed people against their will.

She gave a hard sigh. With any luck, getting some food and decent coffee into her would help dash any more thoughts of cutting that particular angle from the story. Maybe she could actually discuss it with Mel and work something out. She hoped that Mel would be sensible about the whole thing and see the profile as a way of sharing her side of the relationship and the bad breakup that had followed. Pilar wasn't stupid enough to think that there would be no bad feelings; breakups were always messy, right? Now throw in a pissed-off father like Lauden Crenshaw and you had all the makings of a great novel, but she wasn't writing a book. She was starting to regret spilling the beans to Lauden, who hadn't seemed too happy about the surprise revelation. But she hoped that Mel reaching out meant they could have a sensible conversation with each other and discuss it like two reasonable adults.

There weren't many other cars in the diner parking lot. Pilar found a space close to the door, parked, and hurried inside. She didn't want to linger out in the cold any more than she had to. As soon as she stepped into the diner, she was assaulted with the powerful smells of greasy bacon, bitter coffee, and something vaguely sweet.

The diner looked much the same as any generic diner in a movie. In fact, it was almost ridiculously quaint and ideal. There was no way that someone hadn't designed it to look like a movie set on purpose. The black-and-white-checked tile floors seemed to have come straight from the fifties. The front counter was lined with red leather stools. A few older men had grouped together there, heads bowed, locked in a fierce discussion about what sounded like…hogs? A fair?

Well, that wasn't of interest to Pilar. She opted to skip the counter and move toward a booth, picking one at the far back corner. This would allow her and Mel to have privacy when they spoke, which Pilar knew from experience was important for interviews—especially ones that had the potential to go so badly like this one did.

It only took a few minutes for an older woman with a genuine beehive hairdo to come walking over. The name tag on her apron said Dolly. She smiled, pen already pressed to the pad of her paper, and said, "Hello, stranger. What can I get for you?" Was that a twang in her voice?

"What do you recommend?"

"Well, we got eggs, bacon, pancakes, sausage, toast. I can check to see if we have any grits left. So what will you have?"

Pilar looked over the menu. The sound of eggs hitting the greasy grill made her look over at the window to the kitchen. She wondered how long it had been since it was cleaned. So, eggs were out. Instead, she went for something light and quick—pancakes.

"Something to drink?" The waitress scribbled on the pad and before Pilar could ask, said, "Coffee, tea, milk, and orange juice."

She didn't bother to ask if the orange juice was freshly squeezed. "Coffee, two creamers, and sweetener."

"Don't got sweetener, sugar's on the table."

"Great. Thank you."

Pilar took out her phone and her voice recorder. She liked having a separate piece of equipment instead of an app so her phone was free for other things if she needed it. She pulled out a pad and paper. She liked to take notes, and she'd written some questions for the interview. Pilar looked out the window. A clear view of the town spread out before her. It was so different from where she grew up. As the second of five children with a single mom, she dreamed of the country when she was a kid. She loved horses and to have a horse meant country life. Growing up in a fifth-floor walk-up, every kid wanted two things: an elevator and a lawn. The closest thing to a lawn was the park down the street where all the drunks, drug dealers, and gangs hung out. She often wondered what kids in the country fantasized about.

An enormous plate of fluffy pancakes, served with a few sausage links, and the coffee was unceremoniously dumped on the table without a word from the plump waitress. Lifting the coffee cup to her lips, Pilar blew on the heated brew and then reveled in the taste. It was one of the best cups that Pilar had gotten her hands on since leaving the city.

She dove into the stack of pancakes, smearing it with huge dollops of butter, then crisscrossed the stack with her knife and lavished the slices with syrup. Popping a stack of squares into her mouth, she closed her eyes and sighed as she realized she should have come here sooner. Really, she was surprised by how good the food was. She had been expecting the diner food to be filled with grease and mostly inedible, and was pleased to find that it was actually the exact opposite. The pancakes were light and fluffy, the sausage was crisp in the corners, and the coffee nearly divine.

She decided that it wouldn't be a heartache to wait here for Mel to show up. A little more coffee and she would be set. It would also give her longer to try to come up with a game plan. Pilar was used to flirting the information out of people with her smooth-talking style, but she had the feeling that wasn't going to work when it came to Mel Crenshaw. Instead, Pilar thought that maybe being very blunt and straightforward about the situation would work out more fully in her favor. If she explained things honestly, she might be able to leave with both her ethics and her cover story intact.

Granted, that all depended on Mel being more cooperative than she had been so far. Pilar could only hope that Mel initiating the meeting meant that the woman was more open to an actual interview.

Sure, Pilar wasn't holding her breath about it. But a girl could still hope, even if it was for a farfetched and mostly unlikely outcome.

Stranger things had happened, right?

❧❧❧❧

Mel woke up with a pounding headache and a mouth so dry her tongue felt like a prickly cactus. All of her joints were stiff and her nose was sore from the dry, cold air mixed with the sputtering warmth from the space heater as it occasionally came to life throughout the night. Her back wasn't in a much better state—the nest that she had made up might have been comfortable while she was up and drinking, but it had not done any wonders for her spine. Mel was well aware of the fact that she was not anywhere near as young as she used to be.

With a roll of her shoulders, she eased her way to the shower, resigning herself to suffer through the cold water. Hot water—no, scalding water—slammed against her. She jumped back out of the shower, shocked and soaking wet. So Andy had come through. At least he was the one man she could count on.

Adjusting the temperature, she tested the water before stepping back in. While it did nothing for the pain lancing its way through her body or for her headache, it made her feel a little less like the walking dead. As soon as she was out, she blew her hair dry and dressed in warm clothes, trying to fend off the chill before it could fully sink into her bones.

Mel eased her way down to the kitchen, careful not to make any sudden movements that would further aggravate her headache. She downed a tall glass of cold water, aspirin, and grabbed herself a cup of coffee to nurse while she sat in the living room, warming herself in front of the space heater. Everything that had happened the day before was catching up to her now that she was fully awake and more functional. It felt a little more like a bad dream that had come to reality. Her head hurt just from thinking about it.

A part of Mel regretted calling up Pilar and arranging for the meeting. She didn't want to have to face down any more demons, and she knew Pilar would be out with her knives, ready to carve up and parse anything she said. She didn't want to have to deal with this stupid bullshit blowing up in her face. Mel just wanted to go back to fixing up her money pit of a house and finishing her novel. She wanted to move on with her life, pretending that her father hadn't disowned her yesterday and there wasn't a crazed ex-girlfriend—two ex-girlfriends, actually—threatening to rise up and ruin her life.

Mel set her coffee down on the table, scrubbed her face, and yelled into her hands. She could easily just lie down on the couch and go back to sleep. If she did that, maybe the reporter would finally get the message and leave. Not likely with a Pilar Stein type.

Of course, that was just one part of Mel. The rest of Mel was still spitting mad and ready for blood. She was furious that Pilar had followed her here and invaded her privacy just like that. She was even more furious that Pilar had gotten her father involved and clearly tossed her sexuality around like it was just yesterday's news. Just one more thing to add to the dumpster fire that was Mel's life.

It brought to mind the phrase "anything for the next story," which was, incidentally, one of the more palatable and less tawdry phrases that Mel had come up with the night before, with full intention to say it straight to Pilar's face today.

Mel could only justify moping for so long before she let it consume her life. She forced herself to get up, put away her coffee, and go through the tedious process of shutting off and unplugging all the space heaters. With the way Mel's luck was going, leaving them plugged in would cause a fire that would burn down the entire house. Thanks, but she would pass on that.

When every possible precaution had been taken, Mel finally relented and went out to her truck. She started it up, idling the engine so the temperamental beast could warm up while she waited for the heat to come on. Looking down at her watch, she realized she couldn't put it off any longer and set off toward the diner.

In Mel's youth, the diner had been the popular hangout spot for high schoolers. They had gone there in flocks. It was more like a fifties' diner, and she often felt like it was their version of a bar or secret hangout spot, especially when adults avoided it like the plague when school got out. The owner had been amicable toward them and didn't mind the fact that most of them couldn't actually buy anything, often telling them, *if you're here, then you're not out getting into trouble elsewhere.*

Mel had heard that a lot growing up. It turned out that there was a lot of trouble to be found in this small town. Funny that. Maybe she should have just stuck to fries and freestyle milkshakes in her youth. That would have cut out a lot of problems from her life, it seemed.

Mel realized there was only so much thinking and dwelling on the past she could do and it wasn't a time for a stroll down memory lane. It was time for a war plan. The longer she was behind the wheel, the more worked up she got, and before long, Mel had worked herself into a frenzied panic. Or was it a war state? Either way, she was gunning for Pilar Stein. She would have her in her sights soon enough.

The storm had arrived, and it was a Category 5 named Mel Crenshaw. She was ready for blood, and she wasn't planning on leaving without an agreement to end the story, no matter what Pilar Stein said. That was the decision that she had come to by the time she got to the diner. Mel was bound and determined to get the entire thing dropped. She spotted Pilar's Mercedes when she pulled into the parking lot and made a point of planting her beat-up truck right beside it.

Mel lowered herself out of the vehicle and walked around the Merc. She couldn't help but notice the suitcase and laptop bag in the passenger seat. That was good news. Pilar was packed and ready to get out of town. Now, all Mel had to do was help her leave. As Mel stepped into the diner, it only took a moment before Mel's gaze landed on Pilar. Her eyes narrowed.

She felt like she had been dropped into a standoff at the O.K. Corral. Her hand was on her hip as if she were getting ready to draw down on the villain in this epic showdown. This was going to be the last conversation that they ever had with each other.

Mel was going to make sure of it.

Chapter Ten

Mel steeled herself, took a deep breath, centered herself in the moment, and crossed the diner. Despite the fact that the building itself was relatively small, Mel felt like she was outside her body, watching as she marched with purpose to the battlefield. She slid into the booth across from Pilar and met her gaze.

The woman flashed a toothpaste-commercial-quality smile, like they were long-lost friends just getting together for breakfast.

"Thanks for meeting me." She pushed her mostly empty plate off to the side so there was room on the table between the two of them. "Did you want to order something?"

"No," Mel said, trying to calm the building anger in her voice. "I want you to drop the story."

Pilar's smile faltered—just a little—but it didn't detract from her beautiful face. Where did that come from? Mel thought as she tried to realign her focus with her mission. Her dark hair and sun-drenched complexion were an asset Mel was sure she used to her benefit.

"Well you get right to the point. By the way, that was you out on the road with the flat tire, and then again at the grocery store the other night, wasn't it? I should have put two and two together, but the short hair threw me." She pointed to Mel's new cropped cut.

"It's quite attractive." Pilar's lips slid into a seductive smile.

"Drop the story."

Pilar sighed. "Look, I really can't do that. I'm sorry."

"So, you're just a yellow journalist?" She'd launched the initial shot.

"Look, let's not blow this out of proportion. I'm just trying to do my job and give the readers a glimpse into the life of a successful writer who suddenly disappeared from public life. People are worried about you. Are you going through a tough patch?" Her eyes sparkled with enthusiasm. It was an odd concept to Mel that someone took pleasure in destroying another person's life.

"Tough patch? So, you think that it's just a tough patch when someone is stalking you and prying into your personal life?" Mel said, trying to calm down, but the opposite was happening. Her body was coiled tight, and she was ready to pounce if the woman didn't relent. She wouldn't be responsible for her actions if the answer was still no by the end of the conversation, which was looking more and more like it only had minutes to live.

Pilar put up her hand up in defense. "Oh, hold on. I'm just trying to do my job, and a good profile is balanced and informative. Part of that is to go to where the person lives and talk to people around them to get an idea of what the community thinks of them, get friends to talk about them, stuff like that. I wasn't stalking you. It's all part of the background I do for articles I'm working on. Did I tell you it will be on the cover?"

"Does that include hiring a private investigator?"

Pilar's face flashed surprise, and then the cloak descended. "What do you mean?"

"Hey, Mel. How are you?" Dolly asked, pad in hand.

"Good, Dolly. How's Ralph?"

"Oh, you know, he's gotta bring that hay in before it gets wet." Dolly looked at Pilar and slapped a bill on the table, then smirked. "You got trouble here, Mel?"

"Not yet, Dolly. Can I get a cup of coffee?"

"You got it, sweetie. Want a slice of chocolate pie on the house with that?"

"You didn't tell me you had pie." Pilar sounded incensed that the woman was holding back.

"You didn't ask."

"Let's just start with the coffee."

"You got it, hun."

"She didn't tell me they had pie." Pillar pouted.

"So, you really like pie?" Mel smirked at the innuendo. Her gaze fixated on Pilar.

Pilar blushed. So, she did like *pie*. Back on track, she told herself.

"Um, so, you're well known around here, huh?" Pilar tapped her phone. "Hometown legend?"

"Something like that." Mel pulled the fresh coffee toward her as Dolly set it on the table and tapped two sugars in it. "When you take care of the town you grew up in, people kinda remember you."

"So you're a philanthropist too." Pilar scribbled something on the pad next to her coffee cup. "I noticed the high school has a big new library."

"Yep."

"Did you do that? I saw 'Crenshaw' on the side." Pilar stared at Mel. "Or was that your dad's doing?"

"I guess you should have asked him when you were out at the ranch."

"What brought you back to your hometown?"

Mel couldn't take her eyes off Pilar, sizing her up with each nonsense question. She'd been interviewed enough to know how these things went: softball questions that eventually led to the tougher ones. Lull your victim into a state of easy inquiry and then, *bam*, hit them with the hard stuff. And Pilar's strikingly beautiful eyes were certainly lulling her into a state. Damn her.

"I missed the country."

"So, this had nothing to do with your breakup with that forensic scientist you were working with?"

Bam!

"My article doesn't have to be a bad thing, Mel. I was hoping that we might be able to work something out between the two of us."

"I'm not looking to work anything out. You've already—you've already done enough damage," snapped Mel. Her voice wavered in the middle of the sentence, and try as she might, she couldn't keep the sorrow out of it.

"I'm not here to judge you, Mel."

"I would hope not. It's not like you don't know what I'm going through."

Pilar's face flushed instantly.

"What do you mean?"

"I'm not the only one with a few skeletons in my closet, am I?"

"I'm not sure I know what you're talking about." Pilar quickly turned her attention to her coffee refill, tapping more creamer and sugar in it.

"It's difficult being out, is it?"

Pilar's head snapped up, and she narrowed her eyes. "I really don't know what you're talking about, Mel."

"So, that little issue with a college intern in your office was all lies?" Pilar didn't say anything, so Mel pushed a little harder. "It's easy to get caught up in something that you may not have had any control over, isn't it?"

"I've never hid my sexuality."

"No, but it wasn't for public consumption, was it? I'm sure your parents didn't find out about it when someone else told them, did they?"

Where was the anger?

Where was the blood lust?

That's what Mel needed.

Except that Pilar's entire face went soft then, and she actually had the gall to look guilty about it. "I didn't know that you weren't...open about that with your father."

"You shouldn't be running your mouth about me at all. I'm not some damn faceless business you're talking about. I'm a person, and my life is my life."

"That's not how it works once you step into the limelight, Mel, and you know it."

"You don't get to call me that." It was ridiculously childish, and Mel knew it, but she just couldn't help herself from snapping. "I didn't invite you out here to talk like we're friends."

"All right," Pilar said, agreeing far too easily. Where was the fight? It was hard to make the reporter out to be some sort of devil incarnate when she was being so amicable.

Was that just the game that she was playing to make sure that she got the story she wanted? Probably.

But it was still proving difficult for Mel to keep hold of her anger when Pilar wasn't rebuffing anything she said.

Pilar gave a heavy sigh. "Look. I know we got off on the wrong foot. I don't want there to be blood in the water over this. I didn't know that you…ah…weren't open about that. I don't want that to be the angle I use in my profile, but if you don't give me something else to work with, it's all I'm going to have and the article will end up being more of an exposé."

Mel scowled. "So you're using it as leverage against me."

"No, I'm trying to explain where we're at. It's not like I picked you for this, Mel—Ms. Crenshaw. I've got a boss to report to just like everyone else. And right now, that boss is breathing down my neck to find something juicy about you and get it out in the open. You're private, and I understand that. I've got pretty much nothing on you."

"So?"

"So, I was hoping that we could do an actual interview," Pilar said. "Maybe not here, where everyone is going to start asking questions, or prying ears might hear something you don't want your fellow townies to know. Until you're ready, of course." She gestured to the window. "It's a little early for snow, isn't it?" White flakes started to gently glide in the wind outside.

"It happens."

"We can stay here and talk, or perhaps you'd like the little privacy of your house. I thought we might be able to talk things over and come to an agreement that makes both of us happy."

"I doubt it," Mel said. "I'm not going to be happy

with anything less than—"

"Me admitting to an affair with a woman. Yes, I get that. You want me to admit that you and I are alike, right?" Frustration laced Pilar's words. She scooted to the end of the booth and swung her legs out, scooping up her phone, pad, and pen and stuffing them into her purse. "Would that make it easier for you to open up to me? I'm not the story here, Ms. Crenshaw, so you might as well settle for the next best thing, which is having some control over what I write about and what the public gets to see."

That shouldn't have been such a good offer, but Mel wasn't convinced that she could get Pilar to agree to anything less. She didn't want her dirty laundry aired, her personal life on full display for all to see. Jill had already threatened her with that and more. She had pictures, emails, and intimate notes Mel had stupidly penned in her love-induced coma. Mel chewed on her lower lip for a moment, thinking it over, debating on the pros and cons.

Finally, Mel had to admit that this really was going to be the best offer that she was going to get out of the reporter. Maybe she could pull an end run around Jill and her threats and spin this in her favor. That was, of course, if Pilar would truly let her control the interview. She would just have to. That was all there was to it. Putting as much venom into her reply as she could muster, Mel said, "Fine."

"Great." Pilar stood up. "Why don't we get it over with now, huh? That way, I can get out of your hair and out of this town. I can follow you back to your house."

"Like you don't already know where I live."

Pilar smiled at her. "Ms. Crenshaw, I'm a

reporter, not a psychic. Trust me, if I knew where you were living, I would have gone there instead of your father's." Pilar held up her bill. "I'm going to pay. I'll meet you outside."

Mel didn't wait for Pilar. She slapped a couple of dollars on the table and walked out to her truck, getting inside it and sulking. The snow was already collecting on her windshield.

She impatiently tapped her fingers on the steering wheel, waiting for Pilar to come out. Pilar strolled over to Mel's truck and tapped on the window, motioning for her to roll it down.

"Should I be worried about the snow?"

"Probably not. It's too early in the season for the snow to stick, so you'll be able to get back without a problem."

"Great. I'll follow you, then."

The other woman got in the car, revved the engine twice, and honked to prove that she was ready to go.

Mel made no allowances and refused to drive any slower than the country roads required. She didn't want to give Pilar any more time than what was strictly necessary. This interview was the closest to a concession that she was willing to give.

At this point, all Mel wanted was to be left alone, and she knew the only way that was going to happen was if she threw the dog a bone.

Chapter Eleven

Pilar wanted to raise her hands in triumph. Instead, she pounded the steering wheel in victory. She'd done it. Pilar had convinced the reclusive Mel Crenshaw to consent to the interview. She placed her phone in the cradle and tapped it, ringing her editor.

"Do you know what time it is, Pilar?"

Pilar looked at the clock on the dash. It was cocktail hour for her editor. The woman lived on a schedule that NASA would be proud of.

She didn't let the gruff question throw her off. "I got it."

"Got what?"

"I got the interview with Melanie Crenshaw."

"No shit? Well, get your ass back here and let's see it."

"I'm on my way to her house right now."

"So, you don't have it yet."

"I'm following her back to her house to do the interview."

"Well, put your head on a swivel and make sure you take some pictures for the article."

"If she lets me."

"Oh, she'll let you. If she doesn't, just tell her we'll use what we have and it won't be flattering. We don't like to traffic in gossip as a general rule, but sales are sales, and her fans want more. Remind her that the

Literary Times can still make an impact on a writer's career."

Magdalena was good at making threats that shook the average person.

"I got this, Magdalena."

"All right, call me when you've got it. I want to be the first to read it." Which really meant she wanted to shred her story and put her own spin on it. Typical.

"I'll let you know when it's finished."

"Get your skinny ass out there and don't let her schmooze you. Don't let me down, Pilar. Good job." The line went dead before she could respond.

"Bitch."

Pilar sighed. Her conversations with Magdalena were always draining. The constant put-downs, threats, and demeaning tone grated on her. She needed to find a better gig, and this interview might just help her be able to finally write her own ticket again, back to award-winning journalism.

Pilar's driving prowess was limited to stop-and-go traffic in the city and the few times she could get on the highway, so the small bit of snow was intimidating for Pilar. Her one and only time dealing with the fluffy white stuff had ended in disaster. A girls' ski trip to Colorado found her snowed in with only a compact car and four women, none of whom had ever driven in the snow. She shivered just thinking about the hike from the stuck car back to the resort.

Pilar tapped the steering wheel and pulled herself back to the present, focusing on where her attention needed to be—her driving. She knew she was definitely distracted the moment Mel walked into the diner. Her swagger, those jeans, cowboy boots, and hat, suddenly gave her the urge to ride a horse, or maybe just a cowgirl. She imagined Mel sitting astride a horse as she glided across the countryside, hair blown back in the wind, her body rocking in time with the horse as the stud galloped faster and faster, and…Geez, Melanie Crenshaw was doing a number on her head, and it took everything to rein in her growing lust. She squeezed her knees together to stop the growing urge to dump the story and seduce Mel instead.

Now that she was by herself, she could concentrate and circle back, hashing over what was said. How did Mel know about her relationship with the college intern? That was ages ago, long before she was on anybody's map. Kimmie wasn't some fresh-out-of-high-school college freshman, but that didn't seem to matter to her boss at the time. The end of the relationship culminated in a very public quarrel in the office, which got attention from the higher-ups. Pilar was shocked at Kimmie's behavior, as she thought she'd let her down gently. But Kimmie had been more upset than she'd calculated, and her wrath had been fierce. Pilar hadn't taken it lying down and wasn't about to let Kimmie take her job too. Clearly, that was what she wanted, and she proved she would do anything to get it. That had been a wake-up call for Pilar: keep your personal life separate from your work life.

A lightbulb flicked on in the recesses of her mind. This was what Mel Crenshaw was talking about when she said she wanted to keep her personal life private.

Shit. Shit. Shit.

Double standard much, Pilar? She tried to refocus on the road ahead. It wasn't often that Pilar found her thoughts and feelings on a subject so compromised. This article was important, and that was the only thing that should matter, she told herself.

So why was Pilar suddenly so intent on making it something that Mel would approve of? It was strange, and not in a good way, either. Pilar should be focused on what was important to the job and nothing else.

Or at least she should be focused on the road and nothing else.

She was surprised at how fast the snow was starting to come down. A thin layer of white had coated the ground by the time they pulled into what was evidently the driveway to Mel's house. It wasn't the impressive abode that Pilar had been picturing in her mind. She had conjured up some stunning farmhouse, like the sort that might be found in one of those home and garden magazines, with a huge spread about the writer and her house. Instead, the house looked like it needed a good coat of paint and perhaps a talented gardener to get the outside in shape. With winter coming, that wouldn't be happening anytime soon.

As soon as Mel parked the truck, she jumped out and went inside, her dog following closely behind, not even bothering to wait for Pilar. Which was fine. Pilar wasn't really stung by the flagrant dismissal. Instead, she took her time gathering up her coat, purse, and phone before following Mel inside.

Pilar couldn't decide if it was colder outside or inside as she walked into the farmhouse. Mel was busy getting a fire started in the fireplace and setting up space heaters. Hopefully, those measures would take the chill out of the air. As for the chill that had descended on the room...that would take more to bust through. A small consolation was the nice view she had of Mel's ass, which was practically in her face.

Max jumped at Pilar, who stepped back just as

his paws made contact on her slacks.

"Max, down," Mel said.

"All right," Pilar said to the pooch. "He's fine, by the way."

Mel interrupted. "Let's get a few things straight. We're not friends. I don't like you. I don't really want to be talking to you. You're nosy, pushy, and if you have your way, this article will come damn close to ruining my life. I just want you to remember that. Oh, and not to mention the little incident where you offended my father yesterday."

"If he was that easily offended, then you shouldn't have him in your life," Pilar said flatly.

Mel's face went dark. "Well, Dr. Stein, are you offering parental advice? Seems to me you made the choice for me. So, I wouldn't be throwing around advice without a license if I were you."

"Fair enough," Pilar said. "My turn. I need an actual interview with you. I can't leave here without one. If you aren't willing to answer at least most of my questions, I'm going to have to run with the lesbian angle as my big drop, and neither of us wants that."

"Riiight," Mel drew out the word. "So, sit down and ask."

Pilar rummaged through her oversized purse, pulled her phone, pen, and pad, and organized them on the couch. Mel sat across from her in an enormous leather chair similar to one she'd seen at Lauden's house. Obviously, they had the same taste in furniture. The acorn-tree idea flashed through her brain.

"Ready?"

"Do I have a choice?" Mel kicked up the foot of the chair and rested her hands behind her head. Her focus was on the fire and not Pilar.

"What made you want to be a writer? Your father's influence?"

"Hardly. My mom."

"So you didn't get the writing gene from your dad. Interesting. I would have thought he would have guided you on your writing career."

"Nope."

She would not make this easy, would she? She plowed on. "How did your mom influence your decision to be a writer?"

"My mom was smart, educated, and well read. She used to read to us when we were kids. She acted out all the parts, doing the voices. And she was an amazing storyteller—the best were stories she made up just for us. They were lavish with details and characters and suspense. Adventures that kept us begging for more each night. She had a real gift."

"Sounds like a wonderful woman."

"She was, and my dad didn't deserve her."

"I noticed that your dad doesn't write anymore."

Mel shrugged her shoulders.

Something pricked her curiosity. "Why did your dad stop writing when your mom died?"

Mel didn't say anything.

"I imagine her death hit the whole family really hard. Was he just too depressed to continue? Lost inspiration? I noticed that he released his last novel about six months before she passed."

Mel stood. "Want a glass of wine, maybe a beer?"

"Wine sounds good." Pilar double-checked her notes to make sure she had the timing of Lauden's last book correct. Things were suddenly starting to click into place, but she would have to change tack and tread carefully.

Pilar walked into the kitchen and stood against the counter, watching Mel search through boxes.

"Found 'em." Mel held up two wineglasses and a decanter. Uncorking the wine, she ignored Pilar and filled the decanter, grabbed the glasses, and walked back into the living room. Pilar watched the way Mel's ass swayed back and forth underneath her jeans and sighed. If only she weren't working…

Mel set them on the coffee table. Turning her attention to the fire, which Pilar thought seemed to be roaring along just fine, she kneeled and stoked haphazardly, added more wood, and watched the flames lick at the new fuel.

Pilar watched the back of Mel's head as the author stared into the flames. "Was your mother ever tempted to try her hand at writing as well? Being the great storyteller and all."

Mel sighed loudly. "We all—my mom, my siblings, me—all of us made sacrifices to do what was best for our family. Growing up with Lauden…well, it wasn't a picnic, as you might imagine. And he became so bitter and angry when she died. She was his lifeline, and when she was gone, he just was unbearable to be around. Lots of burned bridges. You've met the man. Charming on the outside, but…"

"Barely contained rage inside," Pilar finished. "Arrogant but insecure, proud yet defensive. I didn't get the sense that he really misses writing. Just the amenities that came with it."

"His glory days, yeah. You're more perceptive than I thought." Mel turned to face Pilar, her face flushed from the heat of the fire, a small smile on her lips. Pilar's breath caught in her throat at the sudden intimacy of Mel's expression. The woman was sexy, no doubt, but she wasn't prepared for the beauty that struck her at that moment. The love she felt for her mother, the clear disdain she had for her father's behavior, and the tiniest hint of something… Approval? Respect?…for Pilar that snuck out with that half smile. She tried to refocus her attention as Mel continued. "He was tolerable at the peak of his fame, but when the books stopped, and with Mom gone, he had no use for much of anything besides the farm."

Pilar took a beat and considered her subject. The evidence was spotty; Lauden could very well have been engulfed by grief and turned into a bitter recluse who had no time or energy for his kids. It sounded like he barely had time for them anyway. It was a passable explanation, the grieving widower who withdrew from his literary career, but something wasn't sitting right in her reporter's gut. It was a long shot, but the timing lined up…What the hell. Melanie Crenshaw wasn't going to offer up anything on her own, so it was up to Pilar to tease it out.

She checked to make sure her recorder was still getting all of this, then said softly, "I don't think your dad wrote those novels at all. He just put his name on your mother's books. Right?"

Mel plopped down into the chair and filled her own glass, then indicated the decanter. "Help yourself."

Pilar smiled. Changing the subject meant she'd hit a nerve, which likely meant she was on the right track. *This* was familiar territory, and two could play at that game, one Pilar rarely lost. "Not much of a host, are you?"

"You're not exactly a guest, Ms. Stein."

Pilar poured her wine and got comfortable. She

inhaled the sweet bouquet and then savored a sip before she asked her next question.

"Nice wine. Are you an aficionado?"

"It's a private reserve I bottle at a small place I have in Napa."

Pilar nodded, remembering the vineyard from her research. "Inkwell. Well, you are a renaissance woman, Ms. Crenshaw."

Pilar studied Mel, wondering what made a woman like her tick. Was it success? Notoriety? Was she driven to be an entrepreneur, to create, or did she love money? Or both? What drove a woman like Melanie Crenshaw? And, to Pilar's surprise and delight, there was an even more interesting question: If Lauden Crenshaw was indeed a fraud and bigoted asshole who shunned his daughter, why on earth would Mel protect his secret?

It didn't make sense superficially, but that was exactly the kind of mystery Pilar lived for—and had missed. The deep dive, getting to the answers below the surface. She and Mel could parry and thrust all day trading deflective and meaningless comments about wine and proper hospitality, but it wouldn't get her any closer to the truth. She had to go at the issue directly.

"Your mother wrote those books, didn't she?"

Mel stared into the fire. "On a good day, my dad might string together a few paragraphs. On a bad day, my mom could build an entire plot, well-defined characters, and put in a few red herrings that would make Sherlock Holmes drool." Mel swirled her wine in the glass, coating the walls of the stemware in a bloody hue. "She was brilliant."

"And your dad took all the credit."

Mel pierced her with a stare. "Do you know how hard it is for a woman to be taken seriously in the mystery genre? We get no respect, just look at the awards."

"But you've won your fair share. Hugo just for starters."

"Beginner's luck."

"Your mom was your inspiration, then?"

"She gave me the push, but she didn't write my books if that's what you're asking."

"Not what I'm asking at all." Pilar tried to catch Mel's eye but failed. She gentled her voice. She could see the grief on Mel's face at the mere mention of her mother. "Your dad was jealous of your success, wasn't he? That's why he's bitter. Your star rose and his... well, his success died with your mom."

"I knew his secret. I found him hounding my mom when she was getting chemo for the cancer, badgering her to finish his last book. He doesn't have a compassionate bone in his body. His career came before everything else, including my mom, and I hate him for it."

Lauden Crenshaw was not only a fraud, but the worst kind of fraud: the kind that kicked dogs and pushed kids in the mud so he could get to where he was going. Disgusting.

"I'm so sorry, Ms. Crenshaw."

"Yeah, well every family has its secrets, don't they?"

Pilar felt sorry for Melanie. She wasn't just a wounded child, she was carrying secrets that could destroy her father and his literary legacy. The illicit romance between her and the forensic scientist was only a tabloid teaser compared to this bombshell.

"You can't use that stuff about my dad."

Something about the way Mel said it, her body language, her tone, all said she still cared about her father.

"Why?"

"It would destroy my family, and I don't want to be the one who makes him go nuclear if it comes out. Besides, my sisters still admire him, and I won't be responsible for tarnishing his image in their eyes."

Mel's look had softened as she played with the stem of the wineglass. It was almost as if she knew she held her father's career in her hand and, with a flick of the wrist, she could end it. Yet she wanted to protect him. Why? She didn't owe him anything, not as far as she could see. Family loyalty...she understood it. If she put herself in Mel's shoes, she knew she'd do anything to protect her mom and dad, but they were just hardworking, blue-collar people. There was always food on the table, shoes on their feet, and Christmas presents under the tree. So different from Mel's childhood, she was sure. At least she still had her mom.

"Look, I don't think you owe your dad anything—"

"He's still my dad."

"I know but—"

"I'll answer your questions about Jill and me, but if you use that stuff about my parents, I'll bury you so deep in litigation you won't see a paycheck for a decade. You feel me?"

Pilar raised her eyebrows and nodded. Whoa. "I feel ya."

She had come for one story but had gotten two for the same price. One was salacious and involved a woman who followed her heart, the other would peel back the scab of a wound made by a shitty man who'd built a career on lies. The story about Mel's father was just as intriguing as the one she'd come looking for, probably *better* than the one she'd come to town in search of.

She leaned her head back against the couch and closed her eyes. The wine was starting to work on her. She'd always been a lightweight when it came to alcohol. Turning her head, she noticed the dark skies weren't relenting. She needed to get the interview done and book out of town.

A loud pop, and all the power in the house went out. They both sat in darkness for a beat as if waiting to hear the punch line to a joke.

"Shit." Mel jumped up.

She muttered about having to check the breaker box and vanished. Pilar didn't want to sit on the couch in the dark twiddling her thumbs, so she got up and moved to the window. She was surprised to find that the light snow had turned into a veritable winter storm outside. The sky was dark and heavy with clouds. The wind was blowing hard enough it looked liable to take down some of the branches from the trees out in the front yard. Worse was the sheer amount of snow that had fallen in a few short hours.

Mel came back, announcing, "It's not a breaker. Power must be out everywhere." She joined Pilar at the window and gave a low whistle.

Pilar didn't know whether to be relieved or worried. There was definitely no way she was going to be driving home in this weather.

"This is awful," Pilar said. "My car is snowed in."

Mel looked out the window. "Yep, looks like you are stuck for the night."

"No. I need to get back to the city."

Mel shook her head. "Not gonna happen. Sorry." She almost sounded gleeful.

Great. She had literally landed in the lap of her subject and now was going to have to spend the night with the one person she'd been pursuing this whole time—and who disliked her. If it wasn't for bad luck lately, she wouldn't have any luck at all. On the other hand, the forced togetherness also meant that Mel might open up even more.

Mel gave a loud laugh in response to Pilar's silence. "Damn. Seems like someone's karma might be catching up to them."

"This has nothing to do with karma," snapped Pilar. "If I wasn't a decent person, I wouldn't have come here today to give you the opportunity to give your side of the story."

"I don't know," Mel said. "It looks like karma to me."

"Well, I didn't ask you, did I?" Pilar didn't mean to be snippy, but she had to agree. Karma was a bitch, and right now, she was definitely karma's bitch. She pushed open the door and went out in the storm to check on her car.

Mel caught her by the wrist at the last minute. "Hey, I don't think...you want to do that? I'm just saying, I'm not fully equipped if you take a face-plant into the snow. And while I might not like you, I also don't want to have to deal with you freezing to death."

"I'm not going to fall," Pilar said, irritated. "I'm more than capable of walking across the yard."

She eyed the storm outside. Maybe Mel was right. A face-plant in the snow didn't sound inviting. Even just standing in the open door, the wind was cutting enough to leave her half-frozen. She worried at her bottom lip for a moment before relenting and stepping toward the driveway.

"I'll need to get my bag out of the car if I'm spending the night—"

"Wait." Mel reached for Pilar as she defiantly took a few steps off the deck and planted face-first into the snow. "Oh, that's going to leave a mark."

The snow was deeper than she had expected, but Pilar was a woman on a mission and nothing was going to stop her. She tried several times to push herself up from the wet, cold snow. The more she struggled, the wetter she got. Mel just stood and watched the spectacle play out.

Pilar pushed herself up just enough to clear her mouth of snow. Mel giggling behind her made her groan and then roll over. Pilar swung her arms and legs as she yelled, "Snow angel." Some part of her knew she was just getting herself wetter and would regret it later, but the absurdity of the situation plus the effect of the wine had pushed past most of her inhibitions. Maybe there was a way to make snow cones out of this blizzard.

Mel reached out her hand and smiled. "Nice recovery."

Allowing herself to be pulled to her feet, Pilar cringed as a rush of snow slid down her slacks. "Oh, that's cold."

"We better hurry. Neither of us are dressed for this weather and trust me, once you're frozen it takes a while to thaw out."

"Oh, I bet we can think of ways to warm up." Pilar pulled Mel a tad closer and smiled. She laughed at the face Mel made, a mixture of surprise, confusion, and…was that a hint of desire? No, she must be mistaken. She was definitely not Mel's favorite person. Still, the wine had her inhibitions down, and she knew she caught more flies with honey. "Relax, I was talking about the fire you have going." She bumped Mel's hip and strutted to her car, popping the trunk.

"You're going to need more than the fire to warm up any frozen bits that seem fine now. Good thing I have a gas water heater that was just replaced."

"Are you offering a…"

"I'm offering you a chance to warm up, nothing more."

"Oh, god, it's cold." Pilar pulled her arms around her body and shivered.

"Right." Mel coughed and walked to the trunk, grabbed her bags, and slung them over her shoulder. "Gimme." She flexed her hand. "I'm not sure you can be trusted to walk in this icy muck carrying all of this."

"Seriously?" Pilar smiled. "If you insist."

Pilar stopped just inside the house and stomped her feet, snow littering the entryway. Mel closed the door behind them and leaned against it, her arms full of Pilar's bags. She offered a half smile to Pilar, dropped the bags, and turned her around and pushed her toward the living room and the crackling fire. It might still have been daylight out, but the heavy clouds didn't let much sunlight into the quickly darkening house, making the whole thing rather cold and gloomy.

"Strip."

"Excuse me?"

Mel grabbed a blanket and tossed it at Pilar. "Use this to cover up and get undressed."

"All right. This isn't really what I had been

planning for."

Mel gave her an unimpressed look and dryly said, "Really? Here I thought this was the second part of your master plan to ruin my life."

As hard as Pilar tried, she had a difficult time keeping one hand on the blanket as she unbuttoned her pants. Sliding down one leg and then another, she stopped at her shoes. She flopped on the floor and tried to push them over the heels.

Mel stood and motioned with her hand. "Here, let me help."

Pilar obliged and lifted her feet. Mel took them between her legs and slid one shoe off and then the other, letting them both stay where they landed. Grabbing the waistband, she pulled Pilar's soaked pants off long, shapely legs. Well, this is starting to get interesting, Pilar thought as she rested her foot between Mel's legs.

❧❧❧❧

Pilar wasn't wearing underwear, and she didn't seem embarrassed by the predicament. Mel stood silent, not knowing what to do next. She was rarely at a loss for words…they were, after all, her stock-in-trade, weren't they?

"Like what you see?"

Landing strip was all she could think of as she stopped herself from reacting. Her body had other ideas as it started firing on all cylinders at the sight of Pilar's nakedness. Christ, this was going to be a long night.

"I think you can get the rest." Mel stepped away and sat back on the sofa. Trying to divert her attention, she stared at the fire while her guest finished disrobing. A shirt was thrown at her face, then a bra.

"There." Pilar stood and pulled the blanket around her, her legs still spilling out of the blanket.

Oh, this was definitely going to be a long, long night. Mother Nature had a wicked sense of humor for a woman who hadn't had a sexual liaison in…too long.

"The shower is down the hall, and there are fresh towels in the armoire in the bathroom."

"I'm freezing now. I definitely think I will take you up on that shower."

"I'll get you some dry clothes and put them on the toilet."

"Sure you don't want to join me?" Pilar wagged her eyebrows suggestively and dropped the blanket off her shoulders. What the hell was she doing? Did she think she could get the story she wanted by showing a little—a lot—of skin?

Mel raced upstairs to find something for Pilar to wear. The last thing she wanted was for the woman to prance out of the bathroom in just a towel. Even though she felt confident in her stance that the Lauden story would stay under wraps, she didn't want to test her resolve with a naked woman walking around her house. Her libido was already betraying her.

Jill had set the bar high when it came to a regular schedule for sex. They had acted like newlyweds for the six months they were together. Honestly, losing that part of her life was what she missed most about their relationship. The sex was amazing. The conversation was good, but the rest was sublime. Well, she didn't miss the hiding and sneaking around. Never again would she date a married woman, no matter how beautiful and smart they were. Jill was like a drug she had to wean herself off of, and it had taken the last month to finally clear her system. God, they had been so good together. Why did it all have to end because of a man bent on revenge? She would never understand men. Roger Steele, her father—they were men who had it all and took perverse pleasure in ruining the lives around them when they were on a downward spiral. The more people who experienced their same misery, the better. Anger loved company.

Mel dug deep in a box and pulled out an old university sweatshirt and a pair of ratty sweats. A quick sniff let her know they were clean. These wouldn't even register on her libido meter, so she figured she was safe. Standing by the bathroom door, she could hear the shower was still running, so she was good to go in.

Without thinking, she burst through the door and suddenly wished she had remembered to hang a curtain across the tub/shower combination. Pilar stood under the water, soap running down her body, her head under the spray. Whatever exercise regimen Pilar practiced was definitely doing its job. Mel's gaze followed the shampoo trailing down her body. The curves and skin covered left little to Mel's imagination.

"You changed your mind?" Pilar said without looking.

❧ ❧ ❧ ❧

Pilar felt the rush of cold air assault her body, a signal that Mel had come into the bathroom. She hadn't misjudged the look in her host's gaze earlier. If truth be told, she found Mel very attractive, to the point that she could see herself enticing her into bed. If it hadn't been for the damn article she had committed herself to, she would definitely seduce her.

"I've…ah…got a change of clothes for you. I'll just set them on the toilet…here."

Wiping the suds off her face, she looked over at Mel. "My offer is still open. I'm sure you're wet too." She saw that the double meaning wasn't lost on Mel as Pilar purposefully slid her hand down her wet body. "There is plenty of room in here for two."

"I…um…I'm good."

"Are you sure?"

"Yes." Mel stood looking down at her feet. "I'll put your clothes in front of the fire so they'll dry."

"Thank you. I appreciate it." Pilar turned the shower off and reached for the towel she'd shoved in the rack. Before she knew it, she was overextended and starting to fall out of the shower. Mel caught her, wrapping her arms around her waist just as Pilar pressed her wet body against Mel. Mel lifted her effortlessly out of the shower and set her upright.

Pilar stood staring into her rescuer's eyes. Neither woman moved. Without thinking, Pilar pushed herself up and landed a kiss on Mel's mouth. When Mel didn't move, Pilar pressed her tongue against Mel's lips. Her hand reached up and threaded her fingers into Mel's hair. She didn't meet any resistance at first. Her other hand cupped Mel's ass, pulling her against her wet hips, the towel wedged between them. It was the only thing keeping the towel from hitting the floor.

As quick as the moment arrived, it disappeared. Pilar stepped back, mortified. She could justify the wine-induced flirting and her own brief, indulgent fantasy, but that kiss crossed the line, and the last thing she wanted was to make a fool of herself and her profession. "I am so sorry. I don't know what came over me." She grabbed the towel and wrapped it around herself. "I'm so sorry."

Mel blushed, looked away, and made her way to the door. Without so much as a look back, Mel said, "I need to get more firewood."

Pilar pulled the towel tighter around her. What the hell was she thinking? She'd never crossed a line like that, never. She was losing her mind in an effort to get this article done. Her job was on the line, and if Mel contacted her editor, she would be on the chopping block not just with the *Literary Times*, but perhaps the whole journalistic profession as well. She didn't need to make herself part of the story or tempt fate with dubious ethics. Pilar toyed with the collar of the blue sweatshirt folded neatly on the closed toilet seat and rocked back and forth. She needed to make this right, and she decided she would throw herself and lay prostrate in front of the woman and beg forgiveness if she had to. Oh god, another double entendre. She wasn't sure how her mind had gone from professional reporter to a rutting dog. Mel was attractive, single, a working professional, and a lesbian. All tick boxes on her list for a match on her dating app. Jeez, her mind was having a hard time getting back on track with her body. Wait, her body had jumped the tracks the minute she'd laid eyes on Mel's picture, so that wasn't exactly helping.

"Fuck it," she whispered. "I got this. I am Pilar Stein, award-winning journalist. I always get my story, no matter what." She set her head straight and focused on the task at hand.

Interview. Leave. Write a viral, explosive cover story. All in that order.

She shrugged into the oversized sweatshirt and sweatpants. "Well…" Pilar pulled at the front of the sweatshirt, looking at the university logo in the mirror. "This is interesting." They had attended the same school. Why hadn't that come up in her research? Yep, life was indeed stranger than fiction.

Pilar tiptoed on the cold floor toward her overnight bag. Rummaging through it she found her slippers and pulled out her toiletry bag, then went back to the bathroom, avoiding Mel. The woman didn't look happy, so she would need to tread carefully.

Get the story, get the story, she kept repeating over and over in her head. A naked face stared back at her. This was the normal Pilar, the one that was rarely seen in public. The one that bore the jagged scar on her right eyebrow, visible only if people looked closely. A trophy from an interview that didn't exactly go the way it should have. Turning to the left, she ran her finger along the faded scars that had been a parting gift from said interview. The douchebag sat in prison now thanks to his inability to keep his temper under control. Pulling the sweatshirt up, she looked down at the long scar that bisected her body. He had been a real bastard when he found out she was going to expose his philandering and money laundering for the cartels. It wasn't just his bald head that had earned him the nickname Mr. Clean.

The man probably thought that she would drop the investigative story, but that's not what she did. She was an investigative reporter and her job was to dig up dirt, frankly, the dirtier the better. She had earned the Pulitzer for that story.

Chapter Twelve

Mel stared at the fire, replaying the incident in the bathroom. The sight of Pilar's naked body had sent her libido careening out of control, but that stopped the minute she'd seen the scars Pilar had tried to hide as she wrapped the towel tightly around her body. In her research for her novels, she did a stint at the city morgue. She knew the difference between a surgical scar and one inflicted by violence. Pilar's were the latter. Surgical scars were thin lines from the precision of a doctor with experience and meticulous stitching. Pilar's were rough, jagged, and hard to ignore. The rounded humps told a story of the work that it took to save a life. They lacked the finesse of a surgeon. She'd not noticed the scar in her eyebrow due to the makeup Pilar wore, but the shower had erased the coverup.

How did a reporter get those types of injuries? Was she a victim of domestic violence, a troubled past, or something more deliberate? Mel's heart sank thinking about the woman. She suddenly saw her in a different light. No one deserved to wear those memories for the rest of her life.

"Oh, it's nice in here." Pilar walked around Mel and sat on the sofa. She pulled at the sweatshirt and twisted toward Mel. "Is this a hand-me-down, or did you go here?"

Mel smiled. "My alma mater."

"You are not going to believe this, but I went here too."

"Seriously?"

"Seriously." Pilar tucked her feet under her and stretched the oversized sweatshirt over her legs. "Class of two thousand ten."

"Hmm. Small world."

"Why did you go there? It's not exactly a local college."

"My mom went there, but I was able to go under a scholarship for basketball. Grades were good but not academic-scholarship worthy, if you know what I mean." Mel continued to stare at the fire. She couldn't bring herself to look at Pilar. Her mind rumbled with questions that she wasn't sure were her business, or that she wanted answers to, anyway. But she felt like she *needed* the answers. Women hid their pain so well. Under mascara, tons of makeup, and fake lives lived out on the Gram and Spacebook. All choreographed to the latest music, dance moves, and perfect little filters.

⁂

Pilar watched Mel staring at the fire, wondering what thoughts she'd sunk into that brought that expression of concern and worry to her face. Maybe she was thinking about the article and how to survive the snowstorm trapped in her house with its author. Pilar needed to get her on her side—and quickly—or the night would be an unmitigated disaster.

"Look, I had no idea it was going to storm and drop tons of snow. Besides, I'm not out to ruin your life," she said. "I'm out to try to find a compromise that we can both live with. Considering this new stuff, I can go in a different direction, if you want."

"So that's why you kissed me? Trying to soften me up?"

"I don't know why I did that." Pilar ran her fingers through her wet hair, avoiding Mel's gaze.

"Right." Mel didn't sound even a little bit convinced. "Whatever you say."

"Look, as soon as the storm has passed, I'll be out of your hair and you won't have to deal with me. Okay?" Pilar felt her face flush.

"At least you have the decency to be embarrassed." Mel stared at Pilar. "Come here, make our lives livable and help me bring the blankets downstairs."

Pilar looked curiously at Mel but didn't really have any room to argue. For the time being, it was fairly obvious that her car wasn't going anywhere. The storm might not last long, she tried to reassure herself, even though the howling winds and dark skies said otherwise. She might be able to save herself and head out before the day was over, but she was having her doubts. Besides, Mel had brought in her bags, so she might as well make the best of an embarrassing opportunity. God had a sense of humor, didn't she? Here she was stuck in a blinding snowstorm with a woman who probably hated her guts, and now she was dependent on her hospitality to keep her warm and safe. Yep, karma was a bitch, she thought as she followed Mel up the stairs.

Pilar decided to look at this as a golden opportunity she would never get again. She had been able, through no action of her own, to secure some extra time with Mel. It might not be an official interview, but Mel also hadn't asked for anything to be off the record. Except for that stuff about her dad, of course. But, big picture, it meant that if a bit of information slipped while they were waiting out the storm together…well, maybe Pilar would be able to use it in her profile without any potential issues. She'd need to call legal and find out what she could and couldn't write. In any case, she had time to work on the woman. Never doubt her powers of persuasion.

If anything, this should be considered a good thing. She was pretty much getting a free pass at a second chance.

"Nice room. Is this your bedroom?" Pilar helped gather the blankets, looking around at the room. *Comfy* was the only word that could describe the feeling she was getting, despite the mounds of clothes and random "stuff" piled upon the bed. It wasn't like the stark white and black furniture she had in her own house. *Sterile* was often used by her friends to describe her life. Hotel Stein, one of her friends jokingly called it one night after a dinner party. No red Solo cups, bottle rings, or crumbs could be found before, during, or after the party. In fact, there was no sign that eight friends had been in the apartment at all, save her best friend passed out on the couch.

Yep, comfy was definitely the vibe she was getting.

"Well done, Sherlock." Mel said, nodding toward the door. Pilar carried the blankets down the stairs and piled them at the foot of the couch. For now, they would busy themselves making up a little cozy spot in silence, the wind raging outside the only sound that could be heard. Pilar would let the conversation lull for the moment, at least. Then, when the time was right, she would strike.

Mel, for her part, seemed just as content to work in silence. For someone with such a high profile, Mel seemed strangely comfortable making her way through the darkened farmhouse. Another trip to a different closet produced a couple of jackets, which were deposited on the couch.

"You can put one of those on. They'll help keep you warm tonight."

Pilar picked up a nondescript black Western jacket and slipped it on. Stretching her arms out, it was about three sizes too big. Pushing the sleeves back, she zipped it and pulled the hood on her head.

Mel chuckled.

"What?"

"You look like an Eskimo," Mel said, putting the other jacket on.

"Hey, cultural appropriation," Pilar jabbed.

"Seriously?"

"No, I'm just kidding." Pilar was trying to lighten the mood. She wasn't sure she was succeeding. "All right, Ms. Crenshaw. Now what do you suggest we do?"

"Certainly not try to free the car." It was snowing even harder outside, visible through the open curtains. Mel went over and pulled them shut. No doubt she was trying to keep the heat contained in the house. Well, what little heat there was, at least.

"What? I'm going to need to get home and get this story submitted. How long do you think I'll be stuck here?"

Mel pinched at the bridge of her nose, shrugged, and closed her eyes. "We wait. I hope it will be over before morning and the sun will break through and melt the snow. That's about all there is we can do."

"Wait?" echoed Pilar, unable to keep the hint of delight from her voice. Mel narrowed her eyes, clearly able to tell that something was up. Undeterred, Pilar continued. "Okay, I think I can handle waiting."

And then she sat down on the couch, making a show of getting comfortable and giving Mel the most dazzling smile she could manage.

"I'm perfectly fine waiting here with you. I'm sure we can find ways to entertain ourselves."

Mel didn't respond. She'd let the mask drop back in place and continued to keep her emotions sheltered behind the cool veneer. That was just fine by Pilar. Once she put her mind to it, she was sure that she could twist this situation around and in her favor.

"What would you like to do?" Pilar patted the couch next to her.

Chapter Thirteen

This was definitely not how Mel had wanted the day to go.

When she originally walked into the diner, she was a hurricane force to be reckoned with, and she felt righteous in her anger and determination to put an end to this meddling once and for all. Somehow, she'd been convinced by Pilar to come back to her house for the interview, and while it had seemed like a good idea at the time, Mel was now realizing she had simply let the fox into the chicken coop. The weather taking a turn for the worse and the power going out was just icing on the cake of a bad day. There was no way that the reporter would be leaving the farm anytime soon. Mel was stuck with her in a small, enclosed area for the foreseeable future.

"Wait here," Mel said, then made her escape into the kitchen. Great. So now she had to entertain not just a guest, but the woman who was intent on ruining her life. The thought of it did not settle well. There was a flashlight sitting on the counter near the back door. She grabbed it, flicking it on. The thin beam cut through the dark of the room. She had started keeping it there after the power went out twice in her first week in the house.

That was a part of country life that people forgot to tell you about, and something she hadn't remembered from her childhood. It was hard to keep power going for any length of time. A strong wind could blow through and leave the town without power for days at a time. She planned to install a generator for those moments; she had already rigged up a solar battery backup for her water pump. Internet was spotty at best and could be a lost cause any time that the weather wasn't perfect. It did not lend itself to working from home, unless your work was, very literally, the farm that you lived on. She'd used her phone as a hotspot on many an occasion lately, so as long as she had cell signal, she was good.

In the winter, she knew that it could take an entire week before power came on if the storm was bad enough. Mel didn't think that this was the big storm everyone was preparing for, but a freak winter storm at the end of summer or fall wasn't a surprise. This was just a little taste of what was to come. Hopefully, it would stop snowing long enough that they could dig Pilar's car out before the day ended, and if she was lucky the power would be back up and running in a few days. What Pilar did after the car was freed from its snowy confines wasn't her concern. The woman could go back to whatever rock she'd climbed out from under and leave Mel in peace.

On the upside, a storm like this could have been enough to make Pilar reconsider even being out here in the first place—if only it had arrived sooner. After all, there was nothing like sitting in a cold room in the middle of the first storm of winter, in the dark, to make someone hate country life. Mel just had to put up with it for a few hours. She could do that. And hey, she figured that she could spend most of that time puttering around the house doing odd jobs. At some point, Pilar would realize that she wasn't going to get a lick out of Mel and stop trying.

For now, Mel was content to grab a bag of chips out of the shopping bag she'd left on the top counter, a bag of cookies, two bottles of water from the fridge, and a bottle of wine. It was a small offering, but it was the best she could do for now. She gathered everything in one arm, held the flashlight in the other hand, and made her way back out into the living room...where Pilar was not on the couch.

"Damn it," Mel swore. "That's not good—"

"Don't worry, I haven't gone snooping through your panty drawer," Pilar said from another part of the room. "I'm just looking at the pictures you've got up. Your dad didn't have any family photos at his house, so I'm surprised you have some out. Is this your mom?" Pilar held her phone up to the photograph, the flashlight app lighting up the wall of memories.

"Yeah, about two years before she died."

"She looks happy. You look just like her."

"Thanks." Mel set the waters on the coffee table.

"Your sisters?"

Mel smiled at the photo of the three sisters mugging. Someone had cracked a joke and they'd all lost it, including her mom. Her heart ached looking at her vibrant mother smiling with her daughters. Mel didn't want to walk down memory lane with Pilar, and she definitely didn't want her snooping around her house.

"Yep."

"Is this Jill?"

Mel froze. Had she put up a photo of her ex up? Damn. How could she be so stupid? Mel turned to look and then laughed. "No, that's my cousin, Rachel."

"She looks familiar."

"She should. You probably see her on the news if you watch TV."

"Oh, right." Pilar snapped her fingers. "I do remember her. I think I met her at a party a couple of times." She picked up her wineglass and took a sip, then made a growling sound. "Yeah, I remember her."

It was the way she said it that made Mel respond. "She isn't family. She has a boyfriend."

Pilar cocked her head and offered a sly smile.

Mel shook her head. "Don't go there." She bit her tongue as she wanted to say more, but Mom had raised her with manners, though she wasn't quite sure Pilar deserved them. Snappy, snarky comments pervaded her writing, but right now, she was frazzled and tired of defending her life and anyone connected with her.

"Right." She dropped the supplies down on the little coffee table. "Another bottle of wine, because it looks like it's going to be a long day and probably a long night." If she was going to be stuck with Pilar, she might as well enjoy it. "Here are a couple of bottles of water too." Mel waved the bag of cookies and sighed. "Finally, the icing on the cake, chips and chocolate chip cookies. Help yourself."

Pilar made an unhappy sound in the back of her throat. "For living out in the country, I haven't seen anyone actually eat the vegetables they grow."

Mel doubted the woman had seen a carb in years and was probably married to her fitness bike. Life was too short to work so hard, only to have to worry about every morsel you put in your mouth. Pilar fit the journalist look. Blond out of a bottle with that commercial kinda look—tan, fit, perky, bright-eyed and bush...Mel stopped herself again. "Please. Don't act like the city's any healthier. If I could order a pizza right now, I would. But if you don't want them…" She held up the cookies. "That's fine. It means there's more for me."

"Let's not be too hasty." Pilar refilled her wineglass. "Besides, chocolate and wine go together, right?"

"If the electricity wasn't out, I could cook us a couple of steaks. Before you ask, yes I do have a barbeque, but the wind and snow don't make for good grilling weather and it's on the back deck. I'm sure it's piled high with a few inches of snow by now." Mel hadn't stocked for company anyway. Honestly, she knew she was woefully unprepared for the early winter storm. Her attention had been split in too many directions, and dealing with Pilar and her father the last two days had taken up time that she should have put into grocery shopping and unpacking. The fact that she had made sure laundry was at the top of her list meant that all her blankets were actually clean. A small miracle.

Mel set the flashlight on the table, balancing it so the beam shot up at the ceiling and cast the room in better light. She mentally added candles and extra batteries to her shopping list. Mel popped open the bag of cookies and extracted two, quite content in the fact that she could put her focus on eating and not on Pilar. She watched as Pilar practically pressed her nose against the glass, studying each photo. Why had she made it a point to put these up on the wall first? She wanted the place to feel homey, that's why. She loved photography, and these photographs, which she had taken, reflected her view of her life in phases. Mostly black and white with a few colors interspersed, they reflected what was important to her. Friends and family. Not notoriety, like her father's wall of fame, but genuine love for life and her friends.

Pilar pointed to the photos. "A lot of these look like they must have been from…I recognize a few of the faces up here."

"Considering how you've been nosing around my life, I'm sure you do."

Pilar finally moved to join her on the couch again, sitting down and helping herself to a bottle of water. She didn't open it yet, just cradled it in her hands. "I think that we've already gotten past that part of this, don't you? We've been over it plenty. You don't like that I'm here, and I don't like that I'm here. When I said this isn't personal, Ms. Crenshaw, I meant it."

"It might not be personal to you, but it's my life that you're digging into." Mel wiped her fingers on her pants just because she thought it might disgust Pilar—and was rewarded with a nose crinkle from the reporter. It was actually kind of cute how easy it was to read the woman. Pilar flipped a strand of hair off her face and smiled at Mel. She definitely had the cute factor working in her favor, or was that the wine talking to Mel? She had to admit Pilar was attractive in that seductive viper way some women had about them.

Wait.

She was not about to go down that path. If Mel could have physically scratched that thought out of her head, she would have. She wanted to tell herself there was nothing cute about the woman sitting across from her; even though that word could be attributed to Pilar Stein at one point or another. However, all of her busybodying had thoroughly landed her in a different category, and it definitely wasn't the friends one. Maybe it was a booty call kinda category. God knows it had been too long since she'd been intimate with a woman. Geez, scratch that thought too. Where was she going with all these crazy thoughts?

It was the storm, Mel told herself. It was the storm, definitely.

Pilar leaned forward, bracing one arm on her knee. "Let me rephrase that. I didn't pick you for a personal reason. I'm not looking to put a personal play on the article, either. Hurting you isn't my goal. Put yourself in my place. The people who employ me have taken an interest in you, and I'm not looking to be unemployed. So I guess on some level, it's personal for both of us, in totally different ways."

"Please." Mel practically snorted her sarcasm, but she wasn't sure how to take that comment. She'd been able to keep her personal life just that—personal. Interviews had been all about the writing, the craft, and her books, never her family or who she was as a person. She'd made sure of that.

"Oh, no. Don't dismiss it. Let's be open here, right? That's what I'm looking for from you, so I might as well do the same." The look on Pilar's face didn't exactly tell her she was doing the same. The dim light from the flashlight cast an eerie glow on her features. "If I don't get a profile written up on you soon, my boss is going to fire me and send someone else who probably won't be anything close to reasonable. I have bills to pay. Rent to meet. I don't want to end up on the street, and I don't want to be blacklisted from the career that I love. But I didn't want to run the lesbian piece as the main focus of the article, either. People will interpret all the gay stuff as fetish and make it sensational and more about how lesbians are prolific cheaters, bed hoppers, insert anything you want here that runs counter to the…" She held up her fingers and dropped air quotes. "'Hetero lifestyle.' Besides, I have my own personal experiences that I think we may have in common, so I understand. I truly do."

Outside, the storm kept raging as the wind picked up even more. The aluminum sheeting on the roof creaked and banged about. The sudden sound made Pilar jump straight to her feet.

Mel couldn't bite back her chuckle. She stood up too, putting a hand on the crook of Pilar's arm. "Relax. It's just the roof. The aluminum needs to be re-screwed down all the way around. Strong winds can catch it and it makes a god-awful screech."

"You're telling me the roof isn't on, right? Why does that sound like the start to the *Wizard of Oz* to me?"

"No, the roof is fine. I just need to go up and replace some screws that came loose over the years. We are perfectly safe. Besides, are you making a joke about being a friend of Dorothy?" Mel quirked her eyebrows and studied Pilar's face. "If so, I'll put you out on the front lawn, snow or no snow, and let the Wicked Witch of the East swoop in and carry you home."

"Har, har. With a thousand comedians out of work, you're trying to be funny. Any other time that would've been a good one." Pilar laughed, a delightful sound that immediately cheered the gloomy room. "By the way, that is one of my favorite classics. If you must know."

"Great. I'm glad to hear you read." Mel laughed

too, then took the opportunity to make herself busy again, bustling about with the blankets, draping them over the back and sides of the couch so it would be easier to curl up in them. There hadn't been enough time with the heater on for it to really warm the house up before the power shut off. She was glad she started the fire and had the sense to stack the firewood on the porch. Part of her had missed the winters at the ranch, and part of her remembered busted pipes, hauling feed to the animals in the cold and wet, and stacking loads of firewood. All meant to build character, her father said.

As the storm raged outside, Mel realized that Pilar was probably stuck at her place for the night, and she wasn't prepared to have an overnight guest. As soon as the sun set, it would get bitter cold in here. The house was old and, like most old houses, hadn't been updated with new insulation, so it was going to be drafty when the frigid wind blew through. Mel had been hoping to have more time to do repairs before she had to face the first winter night without power, but here she was with an unwanted guest and a messy house. The fireplace was on the opposite side of the room and the chimney had been swept earlier in the month, but Mel was woefully understocked for food. At least she had a few cases of wine and an axe for the woodpile. Or maybe she would use it on her houseguest. Mel shook her head. She was just kidding. She hoped.

She was out of practice cutting firewood, but she knew the mechanics would come back just like riding a bike. Maybe Pilar had mad skills she didn't know about. Mel smiled at the blaze in the fireplace and didn't remember the last time that she had started a fire somewhere. Maybe the grill at a friend's barbecue at some point, but that had been all charcoal and lighter fluid. She would get her butch card back by the end of winter, she was sure of it.

Once the blankets were as fussed over as Mel could justify, she grabbed her glass of wine and sat back down.

Pilar picked up her own glass and seemed to move closer. Twisting toward Mel, she asked, "So, are you willing to talk to me about anything?"

"Look, I know we're both stuck here right now. If you want to talk, we need some ground rules. If there aren't ground rules, I'm just going up to my room and leaving you down here. There's plenty of firewood." Mel pointed to the stack next to the fireplace as she stood up. "If you need more, there is a pile just off the porch, and an axe. Knock yourself out."

"Wait, wait, wait..." Pilar put her hand on Mel's arm. "I'm willing to set some ground rules. Just come back and let's talk. Please?"

Mel settled back into the couch, determined to turn this interview around in her favor. "My relationship with Jill is off-limits."

"But—"

"Period." She lowered the bass in her voice and set her lips.

"Fine, fine. How about your father?"

"My father told me not to come back home," Mel said. She wasn't sure why. It sure as hell wasn't anything that Mel had been planning on telling Pilar, but there it was; the words were out in the open.

"Yesterday?"

"Right after you stopped by, I suppose."

"Oh," Pilar said, which was a rather sad and

sorry way to respond.

"Oh," echoed Mel. And then, "So you might be able to see why I'm not really looking forward to talking to you about anything. I want the article pulled. I've got enough shit on my hands without having everyone I know calling me up on top of it, asking me questions about my dad. If you aren't going to do that, then we don't have anything to talk about."

"Wait, we just agreed to ground rules, right?"

Mel felt her emotions going off all over the place. She'd agreed to ground rules, even told Pilar what was off-limits, but now she was having second thoughts.

"Look, I can't pull the article," Pilar said. "I don't have that sort of say in things. I'm just a reporter, Ms. Crenshaw. An on-the-ground journalist. I don't run the magazine and I don't have any say in the articles that get published. The most I can do is try to control what goes down on the paper when it's written. I like bringing at least some shred of truth out when I write."

Mel snorted.

Pilar had the decency, at least, to look down at her lap. She finally fiddled with the stem of her wineglass before taking a sip from it. "I wasn't intending on causing any sort of family trouble for you, Ms. Crenshaw. I don't think that I can say any more than that on the matter. It wasn't my goal. I thought if I spoke to him—well, I had been thinking that it would mean I was going to have an easier time finding you. But sometimes, talking to family is all I need."

"My father didn't know anything about my personal life. Until you told him, that is."

"I'm sorry." Pilar sounded like she meant it. "Hold on, he never watches the news, or entertainment shows, reads a newspaper?"

"It wasn't in the newspapers. In fact, it barely made a blip on anyone's radar, and now you want to splash it across the newspapers like it's important when it's not."

"I'm just doing my job, Mel. I'm just a journalist doing my job. If I don't get this done, I'll lose—"

"I don't care what you might lose!" For some reason, that was infuriating to Mel. She didn't want to hear about how Pilar's job was at stake with this article, and she wasn't sure she wanted to deal with any honest apologies.

Mel wanted Pilar to keep being the monster that she'd built up in her head. She wanted someone that she could push the blame on, without stopping to think about how awful it was of her father to make that call, or how badly it hurt. Then there was her hiding out in the country…but hiding away had seemed like Mel's only option at the time.

She wanted the reporter to like her. She wanted everyone to like her. However, this was her personal life on parade. Secrets that were meant to stay hidden at the expense of other truths that deserved so much more sunshine. Jill's husband had threatened to ruin both their careers when he found out about their affair, so her knee-jerk reaction was to run, to protect Jill. Now Pilar wanted to dig up old bones and put them on display like some type of social archeologist.

Mel stood and walked to the kitchen, needing some distance from the frustrating—and intriguing—reporter.

❧❧❧❧❧

This was…actually not as abysmal as Pilar had first imagined it would be. For one, the blankets that had been bundled out and onto the couch were fairly comfortable. Pilar wasn't going to start shucking off clothing anytime soon, but she was certainly comfortable enough not to be shivering from the cold—which was more than she anticipated when the electricity had first gone out.

Pilar could power her way through a lot of things, and had done so when the story called for it. Packing through the Appalachian Mountains in search of a biologist. Not her finest moment at all, but she did it. She'd found a reclusive designer who had been accused of being too handsy with his models. Her most coveted story had been when she'd dug deep enough to find that a revered politician had not only lived a double life while in office, she'd managed to have a love child with one of the three men she'd been having affairs with while still married to a baseball player. She shook her head remembering that story and wondering yet again how the woman had managed to pull it all off while on full display in the public eye. She was starting to see a theme as she put all the pieces of the larger puzzle together. These were all stories of reclusive people who didn't want the spotlight on themselves and had gone to great lengths to hide themselves. She shook away the thought, not wanting to confront that truth just now.

Yes, she could power her way through many things, but the cold was not one of them. She had the same capacity to deal with winter that a bear did. It made her slow, grumpy, and gave her the biggest hankering to just curl up in bed at home and watch cheesy romance movies—the kind where the woman has just suffered a major setback in her life and needs to move away to a small town, where there is inevitably a handsome single man ready to fall madly in love with the new arrival. So, sitting with Mel right now made her wish that she had her nice down bathrobe to pull on, her big fluffy slippers, and an even bigger glass of wine. The wine she could cover, and she would have to make do with the blankets—they worked well enough at the moment—and there was something soothing and charming about listening to the storm as it beat out a thunderous tempo. The banging of the roof had initially startled Pilar, but it quickly grew into a fascinating beat. This was just a little wind mixed with some rain and snow, but Pilar now understood what people meant when they claimed to love the sound of rain on an old tin roof. Despite the fact that Pilar had never once lived in a tin-roofed home, she suddenly saw the appeal of the small farmhouse. It had a comforting warmth and cozy feel to it, like that feeling of going home after a long, drawn-out day, where you took off your bra, kicked off your shoes, and traded out your office drag for the big fluffy robe she missed at this very moment.

She was starting to appreciate that Mel wasn't the worst companion to be stuck with in the snowstorm. The woman might have been resistant to all Pilar's prying questions, but she was still decent enough company. She'd heard Mel had a quirky sense of humor packed behind that dour expression, and she was hoping to get a little peek at it tonight before she left. She wondered what she would have to do to bring out that side of Mel, or if she had lost the chance with her endless questions. Well, she couldn't lose sight of the fact that she was there to do a job, and both daylight and time were fleeting.

Pilar had checked on her phone when Mel first went into the kitchen, and a second check of it now proved to have the same results. No service, and no internet.

Great.

"You would think that they would be designed to work better in the middle of nowhere, while the city is just a given." Pilar tapped the screen, trying to connect again. "This sucks."

"You're not going to get any service on that," Mel said, finally returning to the room. "Not until the storm breaks. I don't care what carrier you have. Besides, maybe you should try to unplug from technology. You might be surprised what's happening outside that tiny screen."

"Yeah, well, my life is on this damn thing. Every contact, every photo chronicling my life is stored either here or in the cloud. So, I can't just dump the thing altogether. What would I do in an emergency?" And, more to the point, Pilar would consider being stranded on someone's farm out in the middle of a mild snowstorm to be something of an emergency. "Ridiculous," grumbled Pilar.

Acquiescing, she put the phone back into her pocket, then slumped against the arm of the couch, tilting her head up to squint at the ceiling above her.

"So, how long have you had the house?"

"Why?"

"Look, I'm just trying to make small talk, you know—pass the time."

Mel avoided looking at her, choosing instead to stare at the flames licking at the new log she'd tossed on the dwindling stack. The way the fire flickered across Mel's face gave her a sort of sensual glow that Pilar couldn't deny was rather appealing at the moment. Maybe it was the wine working its magic again, or maybe she was finally able to just take in all the beauty of her hostess, but she was suddenly more than intrigued by Mel Crenshaw.

Pilar shook her head and refocused on the house. It obviously had two floors, and she hadn't gotten a chance to look around at much of anything. She had been hoping to explore the living room a little bit while Mel had been gathering snacks to see if there was anything she could use to get the conversation rolling, but the other woman had come back with supplies too soon.

It was a long shot that Pilar would be able to convince Mel to give her a tour of the place. Her father had been easy enough to twist into talking and showing Pilar around, but Mel had a smarter handle on things than most people Pilar tried to interview. She clearly had no interest in being friendlier to Pilar than need be. Besides, a flashlight tour wouldn't allow her to see all the things that Mel didn't want her to.

"What attracted you to the place? The seclusion, the location, the size?"

Mel gave her some serious side-eye and sighed. "I've always wanted to move back home. As inconvenient as it sometimes is, I love it out here. The city was just a means to that end."

"Why didn't you move back to your dad's place? It's a huge spread." As soon as Pilar said it, she wanted to slap herself and was sure Mel would do it for her if she offered. "Strike that last comment, I'm just—"

"An idiot?" Mel offered a slight grin at the comment.

"That's a little harsh, don't you think?"

"Sorry, you're right." Mel looked back at the fire. The way the flames played out across Mel's face was hypnotic, and Pilar couldn't look away.

"What was it like growing up here?"

Mel shrugged. "Fine."

"You said you have two sisters. Do they know about your dad?"

"No, they have no idea my dad's a fraud."

"Why?"

"Because my sisters are Daddy's little girls."

"Your brother?"

"No, no one knows, except me."

"That's a heavy secret to keep."

"We all have our secrets, right?" Mel looked her up and down and said, "Or maybe it's just baggage."

Clearly, she'd nicked a nerve.

Mel Crenshaw was secretive, reclusive, and had a sharp tongue, and under different circumstances she was probably great company if things had started out a little differently. As it was, Pilar was left struggling to come up with something to say that wouldn't go rebuilding all the little dents she had made in Mel's defenses so far. Pilar the Pulitzer-winning journalist was not used to being out of small talk.

Finally, she settled on, "All right, Ms. Crenshaw. Can I ask you a question?"

"I can't stop you from asking anything," Mel replied. "Besides, I'm not making any promises to answer them. But I get to ask you a few questions in return. That seems fair, right?"

"That's fair enough, I suppose." Pilar ran through her options in a mental checklist and then picked the question that seemed least likely to cause a stir. "You had the money to buy pretty much anywhere you wanted to live. Why this house?"

"You already know that I'm from this town," Mel said with a huff. "Don't play stupid."

"I don't mean why you came to this town." Pilar rolled her eyes. "Do you know how many people I talk to that go back to their hometowns? Honestly, that's not even a blip of a conversation starter. I mean this house specifically. It's clearly in pretty bad shape. I mean, the roof's not even on right. So, why not pick somewhere that was already put together?"

"Oh." The question seemed to catch Mel off guard. "You mean...one that doesn't need repairs?"

"That would be what the question implied."

"I just...wanted the busywork, I guess. It seemed like a good call at the time."

"Does it still seem like a good call?" Pilar couldn't keep the gentle teasing out of her voice. She gestured to the ceiling when she said it, assuming that the rest of the upstairs was probably in even worse shape than the bedroom.

Though the dim lighting prevented Pilar from seeing it, she was fairly certain that Mel must have been flushing from the way that she sputtered. Wasn't that interesting? Pilar was sure that a blush would look pretty on those freckled cheeks.

"Yes, it does." Mel sounded defensive. "It seems like a great idea. I like this house."

"Well, I suppose...you might as well show me what there is to like about it, then."

"What?"

"I'm not going anywhere anytime soon, and I don't know about you, but I'm already bored of sitting on the couch in silence. If you like the house so much, why don't you give me a tour and show me what's so great about it? Let me see something you've done here that you're proud of."

It was a great idea for several reasons, she figured. First off, she truly was already tired of sitting still and not talking. Pilar was a social person by nature, and while she had no problem spending an evening on the couch, music, television, or her phone was a required addition to the equation before it was considered a fun time. She at least needed some kind of conversation flowing to balance out the crushing silence that seemed to pervade every part of the countryside.

For another reason, if she could look around the house—even with a flashlight—she might be able to find something that was actually worth putting in her profile. A letter left lying around, a picture that could send her to find someone else worth talking to, even a piece of art that could open a door to a broader conversation. Anything that could shed light on Mel's inner world. She had very little to work with unless she wanted to go with the story about her father and her love life.

And honestly? The more that Pilar thought about it, the less that she wanted to do that to Mel. The author seemed like a genuinely nice person, if a little prickly. It wasn't like some of the money-grubbing CEOs that Pilar was used to dragging through the mud. Something about this whole situation felt different.

Finally, Pilar really did want to know why someone with the sort of money that Mel no doubt had would choose this house. It might not have been falling apart at the seams, but Pilar thought that it was close enough to that point to be odd. Not to mention she personally couldn't ever imagine purchasing something that wasn't already move-in ready. Just the thought of it was enough to make her heart shudder about in her chest. She could *not* handle it.

"All right," relented Mel. "We can do a quick tour after I ask my questions."

"Shoot." Pilar poured herself more wine and handed a glass to Mel, who took it and cradled it between her hands, swirling it around. Something seemed ominous in Mel's behavior, and she instantly wished she hadn't agreed to answer questions. What could she possibly ask Pilar that would make her uncomfortable? They didn't know each other, and she definitely knew more about Mel than the other way around. Besides, she could sidestep with the best of them and turn a question back on Mel.

"How did you get those scars on your body?" Mel looked at Pilar and rested her arm on the back of the couch, almost moving closer. Suddenly Pilar wanted more distance between them, not less. She hadn't expected that to be the question. In fact, she thought she'd done a good enough job of keeping her body tilted away in the shower to avoid Mel's gaze.

Pilar turned toward the fire, leaned away from Mel, and rested her elbows on her knees. She watched the flames dancing like lovers, licking at the logs and receding, then flaming up and sizzling when they hit an air pocket.

"If you don't want to talk about it, I'll understand," Mel said. Her words offered some sort of comfort in the way they calmly reassured Pilar. Reassurance, Pilar acknowledged, that she hadn't extended when the tables were turned.

"Got any more of this?" Pilar held up her

wineglass.

"Sure, but maybe you should eat something first." Mel pushed the snacks toward her.

Pilar held out her glass as Mel pulled the cork out of another wine bottle. Waiting for the liquid courage to flow, she centered herself. Since Mel had been so forthcoming with the information about her mother being the actual author of her father's books, she could share a little about herself. Besides, it wasn't like she was going to ever see the woman again, was she?

"I was attacked," Pilar stated matter-of-factly. "It comes with the territory when you're an investigative journalist."

"How does being attacked come with being a journalist?"

"When you're investigating one of the most powerful men in the world." Pilar's hand shook as she brought her wineglass to her lips.

"I'm sorry. We don't have to talk about it, but believe it or not, I am a good listener," Mel said.

"I haven't really talked to anyone about it, except with my shrink. She thinks I do need to talk about it so I can get past it and not let it consume me."

"Does it consume you?" She could feel Mel studying her face.

"Not really. No, that's a lie. Yes, it does. Or it did. It took a long time for me to get back to work afterward, I was just so scared all the time. Even after the Pulitzer, I didn't want to go digging, I was scared to travel, afraid of any subject of substance. So I took self-defense classes and worked up to landing fluff pieces on contract once I felt I could be out in public. Not the work I ever wanted to do, but I needed to start again somewhere. My shrink has been a godsend, and she pushes me in ways I think I'm not ready for. The fear, it's crippling, and sometimes it creeps in at the most inopportune times, but I..." Pilar faltered, not sure where she was going but certain she was rambling incoherently.

"It sounds like your shrink gives good advice."

"Yeah, well, she wasn't the one that was attacked."

"No...but—"

"I was doing this deep dive into Howard Plats—"

"The businessman?"

"Hmm, well, if you want to call him that. I had a source who sent me some documents that gave me some pretty big dirt on the guy."

"Wow."

"Yeah, wow." Pilar swirled the wine, avoiding looking at Mel. "Turns out the guy's a dirtbag of the highest order, but I had to get an interview with him. So, I played to his ego. He ate it up until I confronted him with what I knew."

"What did you have on him?"

"He's a cheater, which is bad enough but not a high crime." She leaned back against the couch. "But he also launders money for one of the biggest drug cartels out of Mexico, and he helps traffic in girls. Offers to help the cartels get the women into the US illegally."

"Oh, shit."

"Yeah. 'Oh, shit' is right."

"What happened?"

Pilar walked into the memory with little help. "I was in his office asking him questions. He denied everything, of course, and then he threatened me. I blew it off. My first mistake. I told him I had told my editor I was there and that he better not try anything. He laughed, saying I was imagining things. He said he didn't get his hands dirty. Then I asked him about a photo I had of him with an underage girl…second mistake." Pilar took another drink. "He got up, walked around his desk, and grabbed my arm, yanked me up. I thought he was just going to walk me out of his office. I didn't see the knife until it was too late."

"What?" Mel covered her mouth. "I'm so sorry."

Pilar didn't stop. "I tried to fight back. I hit him and he cuffed me across the face, giving me this." She pointed to the scar on her eyebrow. "He pulled me to him…I felt the knife go in here." She pointed to her lower stomach. "And he pulled it up, and I pushed off. There was blood everywhere." She looked down at her hands as if she could still feel her warm life oozing over her hands as she grabbed her stomach. "He stabbed me a couple more times." She tapped her chest in two places. "I remember being picked up and taken into an elevator. Then the sound of someone telling me to hang on."

"What happened?"

"I was never happier to have butt-dialed my editor as I was that day. Just as I was being called into the meeting, I was trying to reach my editor to really tell her where I was. I guess I forgot to hang up, and she heard the whole interview, the threats, and the attack. She called the police, and they were running through the lobby when he walked to the parking garage."

"No shit?"

"She saved my life." Pilar swirled the crimson liquid in her glass and took a swallow. "It's why I owe her this story, Ms. Crenshaw."

"I'm so sorry that happened."

"Why? You didn't do it to me."

"I should never have asked. It wasn't my business." Mel looked at the fire as she sipped her wine. "What happened to the jerk?"

"You didn't see it play out in the news?"

Mel shook her head. "Sorry." She looked around, indicating the room with her hand. "I don't have a TV. I mean, I have a TV, I just don't have it hooked up. But even in the city, I never watched it much. Odds are I'm knee-deep in research and writing."

"How do you get your news?"

"Like everyone else. The internet." Mel picked up her phone from the table and waved it around.

"Ah, reliable sources." Pilar shook her head.

"Well, time is precious and I'm a news junkie, but I'm in a three-step program." Mel's smile was dazzling, and Pilar wondered if she knew how cute she was when she smiled. Shit, where did that come from again? The wine. And the fact that she definitely was drawn to Mel—she might as well admit it.

"Three steps and not twelve? Interesting."

"Yeah, step one, don't become a news story. Two, move. Three, stay off the internet."

"You don't have internet? How do you check your email, send drafts to your editor, research, stuff like that?"

"I have internet, I just don't surf it like most people. It's a soul-sucking diversion I try to avoid. Besides, how many cat and dog videos do you need to watch on that Gram thing? I do like to go to the library sometimes where they have these things called books. You'd be amazed how much you can learn from them."

"You're kidding, right?" Pilar was surprised by the admission. Who used the library anymore?

"Quite serious. It's a deliberate choice. I like the library. I love the smell of books, the romance of searching the stacks. Sometimes it's nice to pull the plug on that ball and chain lots of people can't live without."

"I couldn't do it," Pilar admitted.

"Well, if you were the subject of intense scrutiny, you might reconsider your tether to technology."

"Oh, the trial brought the vultures. It was the worst twelve months of my life as his lawyers dissected it. Made me the bad guy—or girl—and vilified my line of work."

"I'm sorry. That must have been brutal—"

"I know what you're thinking. How can I do such a deep dive into your life when my own life was turned inside out on the stand?"

"No, not really." Mel pulled at the thread on the blanket. "I actually feel sorry for you. It's a painful process to have your life under the microscope. Isn't it?"

"It's..." Pilar sunk down and dropped her shoulders. The memories of that chapter in her life weighed on her every day. It had given her purpose to explore the lives of others and bring their stories to life. Often it had opened doors, if only so people could see the person who had brought down one of the biggest men in the financial world—and one of the most treacherous. Behind closed doors some people cheered her, while others...well, they just wanted to see who Pilar Stein was in the flesh. "Like a cloak of invisibility, other times it's polite party chatter. I was off some people's invite list, but you'd also be surprised how many people send you an invitation to the party just to liven it up. If you know what I mean."

"I'm not much of a party person myself."

"No, I don't see you as a party girl."

"Yeah, too people-y for me." Mel smiled.

"People were very interested in me around the Pulitzer, too, but that attention was more from the news set than the tabloids. No one cared about my personal life for that story. There weren't a lot of reporters trying to 'gotcha' me into an embarrassing or titillating sound bite."

"You mean, reporters like you?"

Pilar hung her head, disappointed that she was being lumped into that category. But she had to face the fact that her recent stories were more exposés than hard-news articles. "I didn't used to be like that, and I want to go back to that kind of work. I really thought this could be a real, in-depth human-interest profile, not a hit job. I think my confidence about being back out on the beat and my own ego trying to get the story steered me a little off course. But that's not who I want to be."

Mel met her eyes and studied her. "I might buy that. Maybe. So back to the jerk. What happened to him?"

Pilar shifted in her seat. This was definitely too much her and not enough Melanie Crenshaw, but she didn't think that Mel was going to let this go until she got her questions answered.

"Fifteen to twenty-five. Probably in some swanky government facility that lets him play golf, eat gourmet meals, and plot my demise."

"Seriously?"

"No, he's in a federal prison on racketeering,

attempted murder, and a host of other crimes."

"Wow. I think you've been incredibly brave. And despite any lingering PTSD, you're much stronger than you imagine."

Pilar wiped at the sweat collecting on her lip. What she didn't say was he could be paroled for good behavior in ten years. She secretly hoped that the monster would end up dead at the hands of a bad man named Bubba, in the shower with a broom sticking out of his ass. Would Mel think she was brave if she knew that?

"So…"

"How about that tour?" Mel said, standing up and reaching down for Pilar.

"You read my mind." Pilar stood.

"But it's not my fault if you go down the stairs in the dark and break something."

Pilar hesitated, looking at the fire and then up at Mel. The romantic dance it did across her face made Pilar squirm. "I think I'm light enough on my feet, don't worry." Now, if she could find a way for Mel to be on the receiving end of a slip into her arms, that would be okay with her.

Mel stood up, grabbed the flashlight, and held out her hand. Static electricity popped between the two. Mel pulled her closer as she started to lead the way through the living room and up the nearby set of stairs.

☙ ☙ ❧ ❧

Mel swung the flashlight to her right and pushed open the door to her office. Her sanctuary. Stepping to the side, she let Pilar into her office. An emergency lantern sat on her desk. Pulling the handle, she filled the room with light. It was organized, meticulous, and spoke more about Mel's need for order when she wrote. The bookcases that lined the walls were filled with books—alphabetically organized—assorted knickknacks from her travels, and a few sentimental pieces from her mother's collection of porcelain statues that she'd given to her through her life. They had come home to her when her father had decided to declutter his house right after her mother died. Perhaps the memories were too much for him to bear, but it was more likely that he didn't want anything of her left behind. Mel didn't know, and she wasn't his shrink, so she happily retrieved them before they ended up in his garage sale. Another slap at her and her siblings, which he seemed to administer when he had too much of the god-of-fire juice.

"Wow." Pilar looked around the room. "I'm impressed," she said, walking over to the bookshelf filled with awards. "How come you don't display these downstairs?"

"Like my dad? No thanks." Mel plopped down in the chair and swung around to her computer, closing the lid.

"I'm impressed."

"You said that already."

Pilar ran her fingers over the author's copies littering the bookshelf in random stacks. "I didn't realize how prolific you were." She opened one and flipped to the back jacket. "This is a great photo of you."

"Seriously? It doesn't look anything like me. Photoshop and filters."

"I disagree. It's very attractive."

"Anyway..."

"Got any tattoos?"

"What?"

"You know, skin art." Pilar stepped into Mel's bubble. "I have a couple. I'll show you mine if you show me yours."

"What makes you think I have a tat?"

"Did we go to the same university? Drunken sorority parties, first time away from home. I don't know, that's how I got mine."

"Huh, I see. So you went a little crazy when you went away to college." Mel nodded and smiled. "Sounds like my college experience was vastly different from yours."

"Wanna see my tat? Come on, tell me you want to see my tat." Pilar seemed almost too excited to flash her ink, something childlike in the way she wanted to show someone. That college naivete that Mel had seen after a drunken night had a few girls ending up with some god-awful tattoos. The mornings to follow were filled with regret and some pretty terrible art.

Before Mel could say anything, Pilar looped her fingers into the oversized sweats and started to slide them down. Mel's breath hitched as the slow reveal had her staring at the shapely thigh and hip that popped toward her. The sweats kept dropping as a colorful phoenix came into view.

"That isn't a college tattoo," Mel huffed out.

"Oh no, I got this one after my attack. I felt like it was a rebirth after everything I went through."

"Wow, okay. That's...just amazing," Mel said, standing up. She was surprised she hadn't seen the tattoo when Pilar was coming out of the shower.

"Your turn." Pilar pulled up her sweats and

crossed her arms.

Mel sighed. When had they made a deal?

Damn.

"Come on. Let's see." Pilar wiggled her fingers toward her.

"Fine." Mel pulled her sleeve and twisted her wrist toward Pilar. The simple heart was almost anticlimactic compared to the beautiful phoenix.

"Let me see." Pilar grabbed her wrist and, before Mel could pull away, she placed a kiss on the ink.

"That's beautiful." She whispered against Mel's skin.

Mel stood paralyzed. She closed her eyes, her head swimming as the warm breath lit a fire in her soul. This wasn't going how she'd planned.

Plan?

What plan?

Everything in her brain told her to pull her arm back, but her body had other plans. Pilar flicked her tongue over the ink, down her arm. Her lips gently roamed over Mel's palm as she placed a kiss on it. She laid Mel's hand against her face and moved closer.

"You're an amazing woman, and I wouldn't be honest if I didn't tell you that the moment I met you, I was…I don't know…I thought I would, no…I was thrown ass over teakettle. That sounds silly, doesn't it?"

"Kinda."

Pilar flushed, her shoulders lowered, and she pulled back.

"Wait, I mean…Look, I'm not good at this kinda stuff. In fact, I'm really bad when it comes to women," Mel admitted. "I've never been someone who's chased a woman or read the signs accurately. Besides, you might be confusing the chase of the article for something else."

"Melanie Crenshaw, have you really led such a sheltered life that you don't know the effect you have on people? I mean, I read the blogs about you, the fan pages, and the Gram pages all devoted to Melanie Crenshaw—lady-killer."

"What? Seriously? People don't have better things to do with their time than talk about me? Come on, I find that hard to believe." Mel picked up the lantern and walked out of the room and down the hall, Pilar hot on her heels.

"Okay, I know the whole quiet, reclusive, mysterious writer shtick."

"Shtick. You think I'm playing at this? I mean, I really do love my privacy. Being a writer is a solitary pursuit, and it's not exactly a book by consensus. There isn't anyone offering a hand when it comes to writing. I mean, I have my research assistant, but she also doubles as my assistant who keeps my calendar, types up my notes, books my travel for events, and even has to remind me to eat sometimes. That doesn't sound glamorous to you, does it?"

"Ms. Crenshaw—"

Mel pulled up to turn into a doorway and Pilar slammed into her back. "Could you just stop with the Ms. Crenshaw? Call me Melanie or Mel."

"But—"

Turning toward Pilar, Mel held up her hand. "I know. I asked you to call me Ms. Crenshaw, but that was when I thought this would be an hour conversation at most. Now we're stuck here for the night, so it would seem that we can drop the formality. Don't you agree?"

"As you wish, Mel."

"Thank you." Mel lifted the lantern and splashed the room with light. Great, she had inadvertently deposited them in her bedroom, including all the chaos it held. She gestured vaguely toward the bed. "The room isn't ready, I just haven't had time to put everything away, so…"

Before Mel could usher her out, Pilar let out a whistle. "Wow, I didn't notice this before when we got the blankets. It's exactly what I was expecting." She ran her fingers over the rough timber of the four-poster bed.

The ranch style had been an easy pick when she selected new furniture for the farmhouse. Mel had wanted a new start, a new bed, and…well, a new life would have been nice, but she would have to settle for what she could change.

Pilar went to the enormous windows that lined one wall and stared out into the darkness. "Does this face the mountains? This must be an amazing view. I can see why you picked this place. It's beautiful." She turned toward Mel and said, "You would never know it from the outside, but I gotta give it to you now. The house is amazing."

"Thanks."

The light of the lantern cast perfect shadows over Pilar as she was framed in the dark window. Mel's heart raced as the sensation of Pilar kissing her tattoo flooded back. The oversized sweatshirt and pants couldn't hide what was underneath from Mel's memory. Taut curves and lips that needed to be kissed. Her body ached in betrayal, and Mel had felt the chemistry between them from the time Pilar had stopped to ask directions, then at the diner, and now here at the house. The snow angel, the wet clothes, the hot shower, all had heightened Mel's inner lust. She tried to tamp it down by reminding herself that Pilar was here on a mission, and that mission was to destroy her professional life.

Right?

❧❧❧❧

Pilar watched as Mel kneeled down, scrunched paper, and laid out kindling and logs to start a fire in the oversized woodstove. Clearly, this wasn't Mel's first rodeo, and she was rather good with her hands as the fire crackled to life.

"What's this for?" Pilar picked up the kettle. It looked like it should be hanging over a campfire and not resting on the woodstove.

"Would you mind filling that?"

"With water?"

"What else? It keeps some moisture in the air and trust me, it can get pretty dry up here."

"Are we sleeping in here?"

"Well, the couch is comfy enough if you can keep the fire going all night. Doesn't matter to me. You can have the bed and I'll sleep right here. The bed's comfy and it'll be warmer in here at midnight when the snow piles up and the fireplace goes out."

"Oh. Sure." Pilar made small arcs with the kettle. Nothing swished inside.

"You can grab the water from the bathroom," Mel said, nodding toward the adjacent door to their right as she started clearing the bed of clutter.

"But there's no electricity to pump the water."

"It's on its own solar system. Shouldn't have any

problems. Besides, you didn't say anything when you took your shower."

"Oh, right." Pilar looked puzzled.

"When you live in the country, the electricity goes out when you least expect it. So, if you're smart, you set up a redundancy like a solar battery backup that keeps you in water."

"That's why I like the city. We rarely have a power outage."

"Hmm," Mel grunted.

If the bedroom impressed Pilar, the bathroom was less ostentatious. It was larger than normal, but simple. More windows without window coverings, a claw-foot tub, and a separate shower. Pilar couldn't help herself. As she filled the kettle, she quietly opened the medicine cabinet.

Not a prescription or a bottle of aspirin, just a toothbrush, a half-squished tube of toothpaste, floss, and Band-Aids. Nothing exciting. She didn't know what to expect, but Mel appeared to be as boring as her medicine cabinet.

Pilar jumped as a flash of lightning sprayed the room in a blue light, followed by a thunderclap that rocked the farmhouse. She hated loud storms; they terrified her. Her brothers would taunt her relentlessly and took advantage of her fear to lock her in the closet, banging on the door until her mother or father caught them.

Bastards.

Water gushed out of the spout and overflowed.

"Shit." Pilar grabbed a towel before turning off the water, which soaked the towel, the floor, and herself in the process. "Jesus." Now she needed another change of clothes and there was only one source of dry clothes: Mel. Well, she wasn't about to ask her again. Stripping down, she wrapped a giant bath towel around herself, grabbed the kettle, and walked back into the bedroom.

"Here you go."

"What happened to your clothes?" Mel quirked an eyebrow, casting her a sideways glance.

"Me and the faucet had an argument and the faucet won. Soaked me good." Pilar tightened the towel around her.

"I see that." Mel closed the door on the woodstove and held her hands up to warm them. "I'll get you some dry clothes."

"That's okay. I sleep naked, so…I don't want to get them dirty for just a couple of hours."

"Yeah, but not tonight. I think for both our sakes…you're gonna want to get comfy in some warm sweats and a nice warm blanket." Mel's eyes gave her the once-over before she turned toward a dresser, pulled out a sweatshirt and pants, and tossed them to Pilar. If she wasn't mistaken, a very slight smile creased Mel's face before it was gone.

"Here you go. Trust me, when that fire goes out it's gonna get cold up here and—" Thunder sounded like it slapped against the house, making Pilar jump. She didn't miss the smirk that crossed Mel's face, and she couldn't deny she was attracted to Melanie Crenshaw. She'd definitely overstepped when she kissed Mel's wrist, but she couldn't control the urge to be close to the woman. The faint hint of soap or perfume lingered on the spot of the tattoo, and it was like catnip to her internal kitty.

She brushed the soft material against her arm and shrugged into the sweatshirt and then the pants.

Crackle, bang.

Pilar jumped against Mel. Shaking, she buried her head against Mel's shoulder. "Oh god."

⁂

Without thinking, Mel wrapped her arms around the scared woman and pulled her in tighter. Her sister was afraid of thunderstorms, so she could relate to Pilar's fear. Rubbing her hand against her back, Mel whispered, "It's just mother nature having a tantrum. It will be okay."

"I know this is ridiculous. I've just always been afraid of them. Sorry."

Another loud crash forced Pilar deeper into Mel's arms.

Mel looked down at the towel that had fallen between them. Pilar's warm body was firmly pressed against hers, and that wasn't the only thing heating up.

Now what?

Mel shifted, and that was a mistake. Pilar's breasts were pressed hard against her body. She swallowed with difficulty, trying to think about anything but Pilar's naked body. She closed her eyes, sighed, and relaxed into the embrace.

Pilar raised her face and looked into Mel's eyes. Mel recognized desire. She'd seen it more than a few times in her life, and she couldn't mistake the look. Their hips did that dance lovers did when they connected as she slid her hand over Pilar's hip and pressed against her ass. Mel lifted Pilar's lips to hers and gently laid a kiss against them.

Pilar pushed Mel's shirt off her shoulders and

kissed a path to her chest. Her bra unhooked and dropped to the floor with her shirt. If there was any self-control, it was gone the minute Pilar's tongue caressed her nipple. Pilar mouthed the nipple and gently bit down. Electricity lanced through Mel's body, almost paralyzing her with desire. She fumbled with Pilar's sweats, breaking contact for a brief moment before pulling the sweatshirt over her head. Skin to skin, the warmth inviting, Mel knelt, pulling a comforter off the bed and onto the floor with them, then pulled Pilar down on top of her.

"I—" Mel's finger covered her lips. She didn't want to think about anything. If she did, she knew she would change her mind, so she immersed herself in this brief break from reality. The morning would bring it back with force, but right now she just wanted to let her body feel someone…Well, she just wanted to get lost in the moment knowing she probably wouldn't see Pilar ever again. Suddenly that didn't matter.

Her thumbs looped into the sweatpants and pushed down as she flipped Pilar onto her back. Mel traced a scar with her tongue as Pilar let out a groan. She wanted to erase the memory that came with the damage but knew she couldn't. If she was writing this for a novel she would swoop in and save the damsel in distress, kill the offender, and ride off into the sunset on a stout steed. But this wasn't a novel, and Mel could only hope that lavishing love upon those scars would provide a different association for Pilar.

Pilar threaded her fingers in Mel's hair, groaned, and pushed her head lower down her body. Mel's tongue left a trail until she hit Pilar's small landing strip. Dipping her tongue between Pilar's folds, she wrapped her arms around Pilar's legs, pulling her hips tight and stroking the extended clit with her tongue. Mel was surprised as Pilar's hips quickly began to thrust toward Mel. As Pilar climaxed, her body tensed. She grabbed the comforter, pulling it in close as goose bumps rippled all over her body. Mel rested her head on Pilar's mound, wondering what she should say. Before Mel could say anything, Pilar flipped Mel onto her back and announced, "My turn."

ɔ⭑ɔ⭑⭑

"You've been clouding my dreams this past week, and I couldn't figure out why. Now I know."

Mel's heart raced as Pilar rested her head on Mel's stomach, her hand gently roaming over the contours of her belly.

"I haven't been with anyone since the attack. I was too ashamed to let anyone see me like this. I…"

Mel lifted Pilar's head up and put her finger against her lips. "I'm sorry that happened to you."

Pilar looked up at her with a face full of profound sadness. Her heart ached for Pilar. She pulled the comforter around them and twisted them face-to-face. The warmth of the wooden stove engulfed them, and they stared at each other.

"You know there is a perfectly good bed right there." Mel pointed up.

"Uh-huh." Pilar closed her eyes and rested her forehead against Mel's. "I'm not sure I could move if I wanted to right now."

Mel wrapped her arms tight around Pilar. She reckoned they could move to the bed…eventually.

Chapter Fourteen

A nose pushed against her neck, followed by a wet lick placed on her cheek.

"Max, what are you doing?" Mel pushed the lovesick hound off and pulled the blankets tighter around her neck. She closed her eyes, listening for sounds coming from the bathroom.

Nothing.

She waited, hoping that she would hear something from the kitchen. Like what? Maybe Pilar was a breakfast whiz and was down in the kitchen, showing her appreciation for the fantastic night of sex.

Still nothing.

Bright light peeked through the slit in the curtain, so it had to be midday since it was the only time the room got that much sun. She hadn't slept like that in months, and she wasn't exactly in a hurry to face the day and make awkward small talk with someone who was probably still determined to expose her life to the world.

The sound of water dripping off the tin roof made her smile. These were the sounds of her childhood: chickens squawking to be fed, cows mooing for breakfast, and a rooster who would probably make better stock than an alarm clock.

Maybe they could come to an understanding about the article. Then again, Pilar didn't seem like the type to let a scoop pass her by, not if it meant another award or big payday. Pulling the blankets tighter around her neck, she waited a few minutes and then realized that maybe Pilar had left like a thief in the night. She palmed her head and cursed her stupidity. She'd just had an amazing night of sex with a woman who knew almost all of her secrets. How could she have been so reckless to let her guard down? What an idiot she was. Her body had taken over her better judgment and she had practically given the woman the keys to the kingdom. Pillow talk and wine were her enemy.

What was done was done. She would just have to do damage control when the article came out. Maybe she could talk to her sisters and brother and fill them in before the story broke. Her father…well, she didn't owe him anything but honesty—the same kind of honesty, in fact, that he gave her two days before. He should have been honest about her mother writing his books. He should have given her credit. In her mind, he deserved what was coming. But her siblings didn't. She'd have to make that right first.

Rolling over toward the empty bed, she noticed something on the pillow. Sitting up, she stared at the recorder, notepad, and a handwritten note sitting nestled in the down pillow. Picking it up, she stared at the note. She couldn't help the tears that fell.

Mel,

First, let me say that last night was wonderful. I haven't been with someone so caring and kind in such a long time that I forgot what it was like to care about someone. I've made a decision that I am sure you can get behind. I can't write the article. I can't do that to you. I hope someday, when you're ready, we can reconnect. Talk, have a drink, and maybe make snow angels again.

Pilar

Mel ran her finger over the script. She had beautiful handwriting.

She picked up the recorder and hit play. Pilar's soft voice played through the small speaker.

"Melanie Crenshaw, the elusive writer, has fallen off the map. Where did she go? Did it have to do with her adulterous relationship with Jill Steele? Did it have anything to do with the threats Jill's husband made? Did she…"

Mel turned it off and picked up the notepad. Flipping it open to the middle, she recognized the writing.

"Lauden Crenshaw. How does he not know his daughter is a lesbian? After talking to him, I get a strange feeling his disconnect from his daughter has nothing to do with her being gay. He honestly acted as if he didn't know, so it has to be something else, but what? That answer lies with the author herself, and I will find out." Mel could almost hear Pilar's voice as she read the notes—her tone, her diction, and the way she emphasized certain syllables in words. Pilar was a combination of stereotypes, from hard-hitting, overconfident journalist to erotic woman who Mel remembered squirming under her caresses.

Flipping a few more pages, she stopped at an underlined section.

"He didn't write his novels. I suspected that his wife was the woman behind the legend. But how could he do that? He is a fraud. It all makes sense that his novels stopped after her death."

Mel closed the notepad and leaned back against the pillows. Pilar knew the family secret and could easily have broadcasted the blockbuster of all stories to every corner of the globe, yet here it sat on her bed. No one had ever done something so selfless for her, not ever. Not Jill, not her dad, not her editor, no one. But if she believed the note, Pilar had done just that: put Mel before her career.

Mel jumped from the bed and shrugged into her sweats and slippers, then raced down the stairs. She flung open the door. The only evidence that Pilar had been there was the melting wet tire tracks lining her driveway.

The woman had caught her totally by surprise on so many levels, and now all of the notes and recordings that could have given Pilar a big payday were in Mel's sole possession.

Why had she done it? Mel knew what she wanted the answer to be, but until she talked to Pilar, she was only guessing.

Mel was about to search for Pilar's business card, then remembered that she had called her two nights ago. She grabbed her phone and scrolled through her call log, then pressed send. Her pulse raced as the line started to ring.

⁂

Pilar tugged her jacket tighter around her. The car just wouldn't get warm. That would be the last time she rented a convertible. Damn, it was cold. The weather had broken and Pilar found her chance to escape. She needed to put as much distance between her and Melanie Crenshaw as she could. It had been a truly amazing night, but her heart ached and she had felt almost dirty looking down at the notepad and recorder sitting in her purse. She'd sat on the couch for a long time trying to rationalize the bombshell article that would definitely put her on the speaker's circuit. But which one did she run with? The award-winning author who was a fraud? Or the closeted lesbian author who ruined a top forensic scientist's marriage? Both stories were huge, yet staring at Mel as she slept made her feel more and more like the hypocrite she worried people would see her as. Then there was the fraud who lay just under the surface. How could she ruin Mel's life when her own privacy battle to get justice had nearly torn her in half? Now she was looking at doing the same thing to Mel, and it just wasn't right.

Her only option was to leave before Mel woke, before she had to explain her actions. Mel would never believe that she didn't sleep with her for the story. No, they would never be able to move past what Pilar had done. It was better for everyone if Pilar just disappeared and tried to leave Melanie Crenshaw in the rearview mirror. And that's what she did.

Pilar wiped at her eyes. "Damn you, Mel Crenshaw."

As Pilar drove down the small county lane, she had to admit the beauty of the countryside was captivating and finally understood why Mel had retreated to its quaint solitude.

Her phone rang through the sound system of the car. An unknown number popped up on the display. With her luck it was probably one of those damn companies trying to sell her a warranty for a car she didn't own anymore.

"Pilar Stein," she said, hoping her voice gave the intruder the "I'm not in the mood" vibe she was going for.

"Pilar?"

Pilar froze. This was definitely not the caller she was expecting.

"Ms. Crenshaw?" Pilar dropped into professional mode instantly, not knowing which Melanie Crenshaw was on the other end.

"I wanted to know if we could talk?"

"Ah…" Pilar stiffened. She'd made her decision, and now she had to live with it. "I'm sorry, Ms. Crenshaw. I'm already on the road and halfway home."

"Look, Pilar, we need to talk. I got your note, and I can't let you torch your career like this. Perhaps we can figure out a solution that we can both live with?"

"Ms. Crenshaw, I've thought about this at length, and I'm sure you'll agree it's for the best. I should really get off the phone. Distracted driving and all. I'd hate to end this trip with a ticket. Perhaps we'll see each other at a bookstore or something."

"Pilar, are you trying to be funny? If you don't turn around and come back, I'll just call your editor and hand over everything to her, and she can find someone else to write the article. I'd rather you'd be the person, but I can't force you to talk to me."

"You wouldn't dare." Pilar slowed down and pulled off the road.

"Oh, if you've done the amount of homework you say you have, then I think you know I would." Mel's voice softened. "Wouldn't it just be easier for us to talk about this? I thought after last night, maybe we…"

"Connected?" Pilar pushed her fingers against

her lips. She couldn't believe she'd just said that. Christ on a cracker.

"Yes. Exactly. Connected," Mel said hesitantly.

Pilar's heart raced as she remembered how gentle Mel was last night. So, what were those two choices Mel had offered?

"Pilar?"

"Yes."

"We should talk."

Pilar yanked on the wheel and pointed the Mercedes back down the road she'd just traveled. "We should definitely talk, Ms. Crenshaw."

"Mel. Remember, call me Mel."

"I remember, Mel." Pilar pressed her foot harder on the gas pedal. "I definitely remember," she whispered, pushing the metal stallion to the future.

About The Author

Isabella lives on the central coast with her wife, and three sons. She teaches college and in her spare time, which there seems to be little of lately, she is working on her writers retreat in the Sierra foothills. She is a GLCS award winner for *Always Faithful* and a finalist for *Scarlet Masquerade*. She also finaled in the International National Book awards and has two honorable mentions in the Rainbow Awards.

She also writes under the nom de plume - Jett Abbott. A darker, rogue who's a motorcycle enthusiast and loves people watching.

Like her fan page for the latest in news on readings, appearances and books.

https://www.facebook.com/isabella.sapphirebooks

or

www.sapphirebooks.com/isabella.html

If you liked this book...

Reviews help an author get discovered and if you have enjoyed this book, please do the author the honor of posting a review on Goodreads, Amazon, Barnes & Noble or anywhere you purchased the book. Or perhaps share a posting on your social media sites and help us spread the word.

Check out Isabella's other books

Award winning novel - *Always Faithful* - ISBN - 978-0-982860-80-9

Major Nichol "Nic" Caldwell is the only survivor of her helicopter crash in Iraq. She is left alone to wonder why she and she alone survived. Survivor's guilt has nothing on the young Major as she is forced to deal with the scars, both physical and mental, left from her ordeal overseas. Before the accident, she couldn't think of doing anything else in her life.

Claire Monroe is your average military wife, with a loving husband and a little girl. She is used to the time apart from her husband. In fact, it was one of the reasons she married him. Then, one day, her life is turned upside down when she gets a visit from the Marine Corps.

Can these two women come to terms with the past and finally find happiness, or will their shared sense of honor keep them apart?

Forever Faithful - ISBN – 978-1-939062-75-8

Life is what happens when you make other plans, and Nic and Claire have just found out that life and the Marine Corps have other plans for their lives. Nic Caldwell has served her country, met the woman of her dreams, and has reached the rank of Lieutenant Colonel. She's studying at one of the nation's most prestigious military universities, setting her sights on a research position after graduation. Things couldn't be better and then it happens; a sudden assignment to Afghanistan derails any thoughts of marriage and wedded bliss. Another combat zone, another tragedy, and Nic suddenly finds herself fighting for her life. Claire Monroe loves her new life in Monterey. She's finally where she wants to be, getting ready to start her master's program at the local university, watching her daughter, Grace, growing up, and getting ready to marry the love of her life. What could possibly derail a perfect life? The Marine Corps. Will Nic survive Afghanistan? Can Claire step up and be the strength in their relationship? Or will this overseas assignment and a catastrophic accident divide their once happy home?

Faithful Valor - ISBN - 978-1-948232-85-2

Sometimes danger isn't found on a battleground—it's sitting at your front door.

Nic Caldwell is back Stateside, working the job she was supposed to have before her most recent deployment, and living her best life at home. At least she thought she would be, except her PTSD is always in the background, dragging her back to her tour in Afghanistan. As she struggles to control her demons privately, her public life with Claire is almost picture perfect. However, a picture can't show everything hiding just under the surface.

Claire Monroe has the love of her life back in one piece—almost. She's trying to help Nic adjust to her new normal both physically and emotionally while also going back to school and raising their daughter, Grace.

With all the difficulties Nic's re-entry poses along with the new challenges of being an adult student, she wonders how she can guide them back to their old life while building a new one for herself.

Cece Ramirez has decided that the Army has served its purpose and she is ready for a new chapter in her professional and personal life. Retiring from active duty and moving on to a new role as a police officer on a college campus, she realizes that she's traded camo, discipline, and rifles for book bags, bikes, and rowdy post-adolescents. While she and the students at Cal State Monterey Bay might be the same age, their pasts are vastly different, and the transition from soldier to college cop may not be as smooth as she hopes.

When a chance encounter at a near-base shopette challenges Nic's authority and leaves her and her family in potential peril, Cece and Claire must pull together to back Nic up in peacetime, and right at home.

American Yakuza - ISBN - 978-0-9828608-3-0

Luce Potter straddles three cultures as she strives to live with the ideals of family, honor, and duty. When her grandfather passes the family business to her, Luce finds out that power, responsibility and justice come with a price. Is it a price she's willing to die for?

Brooke Erickson lives the fast-paced life of an investigative journalist living on the edge until it all comes crashing down around her one night in Europe. Stateside, Brooke learns to deal with a new reality when she goes to work at a financial magazine and finds out things aren't always as they seem.

Can two women find enough common ground for love or will their two different worlds and cultures keep them apart?

American Yakuza II - The Lies that Bind - ISBN - 978-10939062-20-8

Luce Potter runs her life and her business with an iron fist and complete control until lies and deception unravel her world. The shadow of betrayal consumes Luce, threatening to destroy the most precious thing in her life, Brooke Erickson.

Brooke Erickson finds herself on the outside of Luce's life looking in. As events spiral out of control Brooke can only watch as the woman she loves pushes her further away. Suddenly, devastated and alone, Brooke refuses to let go without an explanation.

Colby Water, a federal agent investigating the ever-elusive Luce Potter, discovers someone from her past is front and center in her investigation of the Yakuza crime leader. Before she can put the crime boss in prison, she must confront the ultimate deception in her professional life.

When worlds collide, betrayal, dishonor and death are inevitable. Can Luce and Brooke survive the explosion?

America Yakuza III- Razor's Edge - ISBN - 978-1-943353-81-1

Luce Potter lives by a code of honor. Push her and she shoves back, harder. There's only one problem: Luce has just found out that revenge is a knife that cuts both ways. Now that her lover Brooke has survived the attack on her life, Luce has only one thing on her mind, and his name is Frank. Unfortunately, someone walks into her life that she didn't see coming. Brooke Erickson has survived an attack so brutal it's left a permanent scar on her soul. All she wants to do now is go home and finish recuperating with her lover, Luce Potter, by her side. An unexpected event puts Brooke at the head of the Yakuza family. Can she command the respect necessary to lead it through the crisis? Luce and Brooke's worlds are upending. Can each do what's necessary to survive and return to a new normal

Executive Disclosure- ISBN - 978-0-9828608-3-0

When a life is threatened, it takes a special breed of person to step in front of a bullet. Chad Morgan's job has put her life on the line more times that she can count. Getting close to the client is expected; getting too close could be deadly for Chad. Reagan Reynolds wants the top job at Reynolds Holdings and knows how to play the game like "the boys." She's not above using her beauty and body as currency to get what she wants. Shocked to find out someone wants her dead, Reagan isn't thrilled at the prospect of needing protection as she tries to convince the board she's the right woman for a man's job. How far will a killer go to get what they want? Secrets and deception twist the rules of the game as a killer closes in. How far will Chad go to protect her beautiful, but challenging client?

Surviving Reagan - ISBN - 978-1-939062-38-3

Chad Caldwell has finally worked through the betrayal of her former client and lover, Reagan Reynolds. Putting the pieces of her life back in order, she finds herself on a collision course with that past when she takes on a new client, the future first lady. Unfortunately, Chad's newest job puts her in the cross-hairs of a domestic terrorist determined to release a virus that could kill thousands of women. Reagan Reynolds has paid for her sins and is ready to start a new life. Attending a business conference in Abu Dhabi gives her the opportunity to prove to her father and herself that she's worthy of a fresh start. Her past will intersect with her future at the conference when she accidentally comes face-to-face with Chad Caldwell. Time is running out. Will Reagan confront Chad? Can she convince Chad she's changed, or will death part them forever?

Broken Shield - ISBN - 978-0-982860-82-3

Tyler Jackson, former paramedic now firefighter, has seen her share of death up close. The death of her wife caused Tyler to rethink her career choices, but the death of her mother two weeks later cemented her return to the ranks of firefighter. Her path of self-destruction and womanizing is just a front to hide the heartbreak and devastation she lives with every day. Tyler's given up on finding love and having the family she's always wanted. When tragedy strikes her life for a second time she finds something she thought she lost.

Ashley Henderson loves her job. Ignoring her mother's advice, she opts for a career in law enforcement. But,

Ashley hides a secret that soon turns her life upside down. Shame, guilt and fear keep Ashley from venturing forward and finding the love she so desperately craves. Her life comes crashing down around her in one swift moment forcing her to come clean about her secrets and her life.

Can two women thrust together by one traumatic event survive and find love together, or will their past force them apart?

The Gate - ISBN – 978-1-943353-93-4

Valhalla is for warriors that die in battle. What of those who don't have a hero's death? Where do they go? The inter-world is in chaos and has become the heart of the battleground in the war between Paladins and Gatekeepers. Harley doesn't know it yet, but she's at ground zero. A night of drinking, to forget a cheating girlfriend, is about to change her life forever. A birthmark—or a birthright—sets her on a direct path to a woman who claims to have known her for centuries. Not ready to accept her Paladin mantel, she needs proof—and that proof is out to destroy her. A protector by birth, Dawn was bred to preserve the delicate cycle of life and death. Protecting a Paladin is to be mated for eternity, usually without the sex, but Harley's allure is universally compelling. Harley's rise in status to The Chosen complicates things further as Dawn finds herself fighting for her own heart, as well as battling her biggest nemesis and brother, Lucius. Lucius, lord of the Gatekeepers, is out to kill souls moving to their next life. He wants Harley in his corner and he isn't about to let a little sibling rivalry stand in the way, no matter what it takes. Harley find herself caught up in Lucius's tempting promise of power, but cannot shake the soul-tugging love she feels with Dawn. Will Dawn convince Harley in time to embrace her Paladin destiny and save the souls looking for their gate, or will Lucius be able to sway Harley to throw in with the Gatekeepers?

Twisted Deception - ISBN - 978-1-939062-47-5

There are two types of people who can't look you in the eyes: someone trying to hide a lie and someone trying to hide their love.

Addie Blake's life isn't black and white--more like a series of short bursts of color that sustain her until the next eruption. She isn't a ladder-climber in the corporate world. Instead, she works long hours at the office and even at home, something her mechanic girlfriend, Drake Hogan, can't stand. If Addie can't focus on Drake, then Drake finds arm candy that will. After a long week of late nights and a series of text-messaged demands, each one a bigger bomb than the last, Addie has had enough of her Motor Girl.

Greyson Hollister inhabits a world where everything is either black and white, or money green. She's a polished, certified workaholic. As head of Integrated Financial, she has built the ladder others want to climb. Now she intends to attend a business mixer to confront a rumormonger and kill merger rumors involving her company.

Detective Nancy Hill, the lead detective on the Elevator

Rapist task force, has just been called in to investigate an attack at Integrated Financial. She can't quite put her finger on it, but something doesn't add up with this latest assault, and Greyson Hollister isn't exactly lending a helping hand.

A storm's brewing on the horizon. Can Addie and Greyson weather it, or will it blow them over?

Cigar Barons: Blood isn't thicker than water - it's war! - ISBN - 978-1-948232-83-8

Legends aren't built overnight. In fact, they take decades of hard work, long days, and selfless sacrifice—if one is lucky. Huerta Cigars is a result of the combined passion of patriarch Alejandro Huerta, who emigrated from pre-Castro Cuba to Nicaragua, and his sons Roberto and Manuel. Their unwavering dedication to their dream of producing the best cigars made for a success. Upon Alejandro's passing he left the cigar empire to his only daughter, Sofia, who took over the family business.

Sofia Huerta is Don Roberto's daughter, and she is making a name for herself with her own line of fine, boutique cigars. One late night phone call will change Sofia's life forever. Rushing to Nicaragua from San Francisco, her only hope is that it isn't too late to save her father.

Roberto Huerta, Jr. might be a Huerta in name, but his womanizing, drinking, and carefree lifestyle have kept him at arm's length from his father. RJ think's his father's freak accident will leave him as the rightful heir of the family empire. He couldn't have been more wrong.

A turn of events will pit brother against sister as they fight for control of the Huerta empire. Sometimes secrets and lies aren't the only thing living in the closet, and there is only one Huerta that can continue the family legacy of excellence in this romantic mystery with a twist.

In Cigar Barons, blood isn't thicker than water—it's war.

Writing as Jett Abbott

Scarlet Masquerade - ISBN - 978-0-982860-81-6

What do you say to the woman you thought died over a century ago? Will time heal all wounds or does it just allow them to fester and grow? A.J. Locke has lived over two centuries and works like a demon, both figuratively and literally. As the owner of a successful pharmaceutical company that specializes in blood research, she has changed the way she can live her life. Wanting for nothing, she has smartly compartmentalized her life so that when she needs to, she can pick up and start all over again, which happens every twenty years or so. Love is not an emotion A.J. spends much time on. Since losing the love of her life to the plague one hundred fifty years ago, she vowed to never travel down that road again. That isn't to say she doesn't have women when she wants them, she just wants them on her terms and that doesn't involve a long term commitment.

A.J.'s cool veneer is peeled back when she sees the love of her life in a lesbian bar, in the same town, in the same day and time in which she lives. Is her mind playing tricks on her? If not, how did Clarissa survive the plague when she had made A.J. promise never to change her?

Clarissa Graham is a university professor who has lived an obscure life teaching English literature. She has made it a point to stay off the radar and never become involved with anything that resembles her past life. Every once in a while Clarissa has an itch that needs to be scratched, so she finds an out of the way location to scratch it. She keeps her personal life separate from her professional one, and in doing so she is able to keep her secrets to herself. Suddenly, her life is turned upside down when someone tries to kill her. She finds herself in the middle of an assassination plot with no idea who wants her dead.

Scarlet Assassin - ISBN - 978-1-939062-36-9

Selene Hightower is a killer for hire. A vampire who walks in both the light and the darkness, but lately darkness has a stronger pull. Her unfinished business could cost her the ability to live in the light, throwing her permanently back into the black ink of evil.

Doctor Francesca Swartz led a boring life filled with test tubes, blood trials, and work. One exploratory night, in a world of leather and torture, she is intrigued by a dark and solitary soul. She surrenders to temptation and the desire to experience something new, only to discover that it might alter her life forever.

Will Selene allow the light to win over the darkness threatening the edges of her life? Two women wonder if they can co-exist despite vast differences, as worlds collide and threaten to destroy any hope of happiness. Who will win?

Other Sapphire books from Sapphire Authors

Thundering Pines – ISBN – 978-1-952270-58-1

Returning to her hometown was the last thing Brianna Goodwin wanted to do. She and her mom had left Flower Hills under a cloud of secrecy and shame when she was ten years old. Her life is different now. She has a high-powered career, a beautiful girlfriend, and a trendy life in Chicago.

Upon her estranged father's death, she reluctantly agrees to attend the reading of his will. It should be simple—settle his estate and return to her life in the city—but nothing has ever been simple when it comes to Donald Goodwin.

Dani Thorton, the down-to-earth manager of Thundering Pines, is confused when she's asked to attend the reading of the will of her longtime employer. She fears that her simple, although secluded life will be interrupted by the stylish daughter who breezes into town.

When a bombshell is revealed at the meeting, two women seemingly so different are thrust together. Maybe they'll discover they have more in common than they think.

Diva – ISBN – 978-1-952270-10-9

What if...you were offered a part-time job as the personal assistant to someone you have idolized for years? Meg Ellis has just completed the school year as a nurse in the Santa Fe school system. It isn't her first choice of profession, but a medical problem derailed her musical career years ago. The breakup of a bad relationship is still painful. The loving support from her close-knit family and good friends has buoyed her spirits, but longing still lurks below the surface. She can't forget the intoxicating allure of the beautiful diva who haunts her dreams.

Nicole Bernard is a rising star in the world of opera, adored by fans around the globe. When Meg learns that Nicole is headlining a new production at the renowned New Mexico outdoor pavilion—and then is asked to accept a job offer to be her personal assistant—she is beside herself. After a short time learning the routine and reining in her hormones, Meg discovers that Nicole's family will be visiting for the opening. Her responsibility to the charismatic singer immediately becomes more difficult when Nicole's young husband Mario shows up and threatens the comfortable rapport between Meg and the prima donna.

The two women brace for a roller-coaster interlude composed by fate. Will the warm days and cool nights, the breathtaking scenery, and the romance of the music create summer love? A heartbreaking game? Or something very special?

Keeping Secrets – ISBN – 978-1-952270-04-8

What would you do if, after finally finding the woman of your dreams, she suddenly leaves to fight in the Civil War?

It's 1863, and Elizabeth Hepscott has resigned herself to a life of monotonous boredom far from the battlefields as the wife of a Missouri rancher. Her fate changes when she travels with her brother to Kentucky to help him join the Union Army. On a whim, she poses as his little brother and is bullied into enlisting, as well. Reluctantly pulled into a new destiny, a lark decision quickly cascades into mortal danger.

While Elizabeth's life has made a drastic U-turn, Charlie Schweicher, heiress to a glass-making fortune, is still searching for the only thing money can't buy.

A chance encounter drastically changes everything for both of them. Will Charlie find the love she's longed for, or will the war take it all away?

Encore Performance - ISBN - 978-1-952270-52-9

Grey Rickman, a journalist for The New York Times, is offered the opportunity of a lifetime and a huge boost to her career—ghostwriting a memoir for one of the world's most beloved actors. She is deeply in love with her girlfriend, dancer Christian Scott, and her world couldn't be better.

Christian, though proud of Grey and all that she's accomplished, is facing her own career dilemma. All she's ever wanted to do is perform and create, her body her kinetic canvas. But, in one of the few industries where youth matters above all else, her time is coming to make decisions that no woman in her mid-thirties should have to make: is it time to retire?

As the career of one begins to explode into the stratosphere and the other's implodes after a career-ending injury that makes any retirement discussion irrelevant, Grey and Christian begin to drift apart. Changing priorities and newly built walls lead to fears and accusations, further tearing at the fabric of the love they've worked years to create.

Will cooler heads prevail to warm up the hearts of the deeply passionate couple in time to create a new dream for their second act?